BOTH
SIDES
OF
TIME

Also by Caroline B. Cooney

Driver's Ed
The Face on the Milk Carton
Whatever Happened to Janie?
Twenty Pageants Later
Among Friends
Camp Girl-Meets-Boy
Camp Reunion
Family Reunion
Don't Blame the Music
The Girl Who Invented Romance
Operation: Homefront

BOTH SIDES OF TIME

Caroline B. Cooney

Delacorte Press

With special thanks to Sherri Zolt

Published by
Delacorte Press
Bantam Doubleday Dell Publishing Group, Inc.
1540 Broadway
New York, New York 10036

Library of Congress Cataloging-in-Publication Data

Cooney, Caroline B.
Both sides of time / Caroline B. Cooney.
p.   cm.
Summary: Teenage Annie Lockwood, wishing she could
have lived a hundred years ago in a more romantic time, finds
herself in the 1890s and it is indeed romantic—and very painful.
ISBN 0-385-32174-0
[1. Space and time—Fiction.]   I. Title.
PZ7.C7834Bo   1995
[Fic]—dc20
94-32538   CIP   AC

The text of this book is set in 12-point Berkeley Book.

Book design by Patrice Sheridan

Manufactured in the United States of America

August 1995

10   9   8   7   6   5   4   3   2   1

FOR DORIE

CHAPTER 1

It was Annie's agenda that summer to convert her boy-friend, Sean, into a romantic man. It would not be easy, everyone agreed on that. Sean was far more likely to be holding metric wrenches than a bouquet of roses for Annie.

Annie did not know why she went out with Sean. (Not that you could call it "going out." It was "going to.")

Sean's spare time involved the repair of mechanical objects, or preventive maintenance on mechanical objects. There was always a lawn mower whose engine must be rebuilt, or an '83 pickup truck acquired in a trade whose every part must be replaced.

Annie would arrive at the spot where Sean was currently restoring a vehicle. She would watch. She would buy Cokes. Eventually Sean would say he had to do something else now, so good-bye.

Nevertheless, on this, the last half day of school, Annie had planned to hold hands for cameras, immortalized as boyfriend and girlfriend. But Sean—the least-romantic handsome boy in America—had skipped.

The girls met in front of the mirrors, of course, to compare white dresses and fix each other's hair. Usually everybody dressed sloppily. It was almost embarrassing to look good for a change. Annie Lockwood had gotten her white dress when she was bridesmaid in a garden wedding last year. Embroidered with a thousand starry white flowers, the skirt had a great deal of cloth in it, swirling when she walked. At least the dress was perfect for romance.

Everybody was exuberant and giddy. The moment school was exchanged for summer, they'd converge on the beach for a party that would last all afternoon and evening.

Annie brushed her thick dark hair into a ponytail and spread a white lace scrunchy in her right hand to hold it.

"So where is the Romance Champion?" asked her best friend, Heather.

"He's at the Mansion," Annie explained, "getting his cars ready to drive away."

Sean would be at the old Stratton Mansion, getting his stuff off the grounds before demolition.

Sean loved destruction. Even though it was his own home being torn down, Sean didn't care. He couldn't wait to see the wrecking balls in action. It was Annie who wept for the Mansion.

2

The town had decided to rip it down. They were right, of course. Nobody had maintained the Mansion. Kids had been rollerskating in the ballroom for decades. Roof leaks from the soaring towers had traveled down three floors and ruined every inch of plaster. To the town, it was just a looming, dangerous hulk.

But oh, Annie Lockwood loved the Mansion.

The girls hurried out of the bathroom at the same second, not fitting, so they had to gather their skirts and giggle and launch themselves through the door again. The whole half day was silly and frivolous. Annie decided she was good at silly and frivolous, and it was a shame they didn't get to behave that way more often. School ended with hugs, and seniors got weepy and the freshmen vanished, which was the only decent thing for ninth graders to do, and everybody shouted back and forth about the afternoon plans.

"See you at the beach," called Heather.

Annie nodded. "First I have to collect Sean."

"Good luck."

That Sean would agree to play beach volleyball when he had a car repair deadline was highly unlikely. But Annie would certainly try.

When the school bus dropped her off, she didn't even go into the house to change her clothes, but retrieved her bike from the garage and started pedaling. The frothy white dress billowed out behind her in fat white balloons. It was a ridiculous thing to bicycle in. She pulled off the scrunchy and let her hair fly too. Her hair was dark and romantic against the white of her dress.

I'm going to ruin the dress, she thought. I should have changed into jeans, especially when I know perfectly well Sean is just changing the oil on some car and he'll want me to help.

I'll help you, she promised the absent Sean. I will repair your entire personality, you lucky guy. By the end of summer, you will have worth.

Lately, Annie had been reading every advice column in existence: Ann Landers, Dear Abby, Miss Manners. She'd become unusually hooked on radio and television talk shows. She knew two things now:

A. You weren't supposed to try to change other people. It didn't work and afterward they hated you.
B. Mind Your Own Business.

Of course nobody ever obeyed those two rules; it would take all the fun out of life. Annie had no intention whatsoever of following either A or B.

She pedaled through the village toward Stratton Point. The land was solid with houses. Hardly a village now that eighty thousand people lived here, but the residents, most of whom had moved from New York City, liked to pretend they were rural.

It was very warm, but the breeze was not friendly. The sky darkened. They were in for a good storm. (Her father always called a storm "good.") Annie thought about the impending thunderstorm at home, and then decided not to think about it.

Passing the last house, she crossed the narrow spit

of land, two cars wide, that led to Stratton Point. Sometime in the 1880s, a railroad baron had built his summer "cottage" on an island a few hundred yards from shore. He created a yacht basin, so he could commute to New York City, and then built a causeway, so his family could ride in their splendid monogrammed carriage to the village ice cream parlor. He added a magnificent turreted bathhouse down by a stretch of soft white sand, and a carriage house, stables, an echo house, and even a decorative lighthouse with a bell tower instead of warnings.

Decades after the parties ceased and nobody was there to have afternoon tea or play croquet, the Mansion was divided into nine apartments and the six hundred acres of Stratton Point became a town park. The bathhouse was used by the public now. The Garden Club reclaimed the walled gardens, and where Mr. Stratton's single yacht had once been docked, hundreds of tiny boats cluttered the placid water. Day campers detoured by the echo house to scream forbidden words and listen to them come back. *I* didn't say it, they would protest happily.

The nine apartments were occupied by town crew, including Sean's father, whose job it was to keep up roads and parks and storm drains. Nobody kept the Mansion up.

Annie pedaled past parking lots, picnic areas and tennis courts, past Sunfishes and Bluejays waiting to be popped into the water, past the beach where the graduating class was gathering in spite of the look of the sky. She passed the holly gardens and the nature paths, more parking lots, woods, sand, meadow, and finally, the bottom of the Great Hill. The huge brown-shingled mansion cast its three-towered shadow over the Hill.

Pity the horses that had had to drag heavy carriages up this steep curve. Biking up was very difficult. There were days when Annie could do it, and days she couldn't.

This was a day she could.

Stretching up into the hot angry clouds, the Mansion's copper trimmed towers glimmered angrily, as if they knew they were shortly to die. Annie shivered in the heat, vaguely afraid of the shadows, steering around them to stay in the sun.

Sean would be parked on the turnaround, getting his nonworking vehicles working enough to be driven away before the demolition crew blocked access to the Mansion.

At the crest of the Great Hill, the old drive circled a vast garden occupied by nonworking fountains and still valiant peonies and roses. There was Sean, flawless in white T-shirt and indigo jeans, unaware that his girlfriend had arrived. Derelict vehicles were so much more interesting than girls.

It won't work, she thought dismally. I can't change Sean. Either I take him the way he is, or I don't take him.

Annie wanted the kind of romance that must have happened in the Mansion back when Hiram Stratton made millions in railroads, and fought unions, and married four times, and gave parties so grand even the newspapers in London, England, wrote about them.

She imagined Sean in starched white collar, gold cuff links and black tails, dancing in a glittering ballroom, gallant to every beautiful woman over whose hand he bowed.

No.

Never happen.

I am a romantic in the wrong century, she thought. I live in the 1990s. I should be in the 1890s. I bet I could have found true love a hundred years ago. Look at Sean. All I'm going to find around here is true grease.

Annie stood straddling the bike, and leaned against a stone pillar to catch her breath.

The first falling happened.

It was a terrible black sensation: that hideous feeling she had when she was almost asleep but her body snapped away from sleep, as if falling asleep really did involve a fall, and some nights her body didn't want to go. It was always scary to fall when you were flat on the mattress. It was far, far scarier to fall here on the grass, staring at Sean.

Her fingertips scraped the harsh stones of the wall. She couldn't grab hold of them—they raced by her, going up as she went down. She fell so hard, so deeply, she expected to find herself at the bottom of some cliff, dashed upon the rocks. She arched her body, trying to protect herself, trying to tuck in, trying to cry out—

—and it stopped.

Stopped completely.

Nothing had fallen. Not Annie, not her bike, not the sky.

She was fine.

Sean was still kneeling beside his engine block, having heard no cry and worried no worries.

Did my heart work too hard coming up the drive? thought Annie. Did I half faint? I didn't even skip breakfast.

The hot wind picked up Annie's hair in its sweaty fingers. Yanking her hair, the wind circled to get a tighter grip. She grabbed her hair back, making a ponytail in her fist and holding it.

Just a breeze, she said to herself. Her heart was racing.

There was something wrong with the day, or something wrong with her.

"Hey, ASL!" yelled Sean, spotting her at last. Sean referred to everything by letter. He drove an MG, listened to CDs, watched MTV, did his A-II homework.

Annie's real name, depressingly, was Anna Sophia. Every September, she asked herself if this school year she wanted to be called Anna Sophia, and every September it seemed more appealing to go to court and get a legal name change to Annie.

Sean had adopted her initials and called her ASL. Everybody thought it was romantic. Only Annie knew that Sean's romance was with the alphabet.

When she let go of her hair, the wind recaptured it.

The leaves on the old oak trees did not move, but her hair swirled horizontally as if she were still biking.

For a strange sliding moment, she saw no decrepit

old cars under the porte cochere, but matched chestnut horses with black manes and tails. They were alive, those horses, flicking their tails and stamping heavily. She could smell the distinctive stable perfume of sweating animals.

What is going on here? she thought.

"They've sold the marble floors, the fireplace mantels and the carvings on the staircase, ASL," said Sean happily. "Antique lovers love this place. Town's probably going to get enough money from the fixtures to pay for demolishing it."

It was so like Sean not to notice her dress, not to comment on the last day of school, and not to care that good things were ending forever.

She climbed the high steps onto the covered porch. The immense double oak doors were so heavy she always felt there should be a manservant to hold them for her. Of course, the doors were padlocked now, the windows boarded up, and—

The doors were not padlocked. The handles turned. What a gift! Annie slid inside.

The front hall still had its marble floors, giant black and white squares like a huge cruel chess game. Antique dealers had taken the gryphons from the staircase—little walnut madmen foaming at the mouth—but nobody had yet touched the mirrors. The house was heavily mirrored, each mirror a jagged collection of triangles, like the facets of diamonds. Fragments of mirror dismembered Annie. Her hands, her face, her dress were reflected a thousand times a thousand.

It was not as dark inside as she'd expected it to be. Light from stairwells and light wells filled the house.

This is the last time I'll ever be inside, she thought, going overboard emotionally, as if this were also her Last Visit to the Lockwood Family As It Ought to Be.

Don't think about home, she ordered herself. Don't dwell on it, because what can you do? Mind Your Own Business. That's the rule, everybody agrees.

Outdoors the rain arrived, huge and heavy. Not water falling from the sky, but thrown from the sky, angry gods taking aim. She expected Sean to come inside with her, but of course he didn't. He angled his body beneath the porte cochere and went on doing whatever mechanical thing he was doing.

Annie resolved to find a boyfriend with interests other than cars and sound systems. He'd be incredibly gorgeous and romantic, plus entranced by Annie.

The stairs loomed darkly.

These were stairs for trailing ballgowns and elbow length white gloves, the sweet scent of lilac perfume wafting as you rested your fragile hand on the arm of your betrothed.

It was difficult to think of Sean ever becoming a girl's betrothed. Sean had a hard time taking Annie to the movies, never mind getting engaged. He was the sort who would stay in love with cars and trucks, and end up married quite accidentally, without noticing.

Annie walked into the ballroom. Circular, with wooden floors, it had been destroyed by decades of tenants' children's birthday parties. The upholstery on its many window seats was long gone. Only the tack holes remained.

I wish I could see the Mansion the way it was. I wish I could be here a hundred years ago and have what they had, dress as they dressed, live as they lived.

Oh, she knew what they had had: smallpox and tuberculosis and no anesthesia for childbirth. No contact lenses, no movies, no shopping malls, no hamburgers. Still, how nice to have both centuries . . . the way her father was having both women.

I try not to hate him, or Miss Bartten either, she thought, but how do I do that? My mother is this wonderful woman, who loves her family, loves her job, loves her house—and Daddy forgets her? Falls in love with the new gym teacher at the high school where he teaches music?

The musical Daddy had put on last year was *West Side Story,* which he'd postponed for years because you had to have boys who were excellent dancers. There was no such thing.

But when Miss Bartten joined the faculty, she convinced the football coach that the boys needed to study dance for agility and coordination, and now had in the palm of her hand a dozen big terrific boys who could dance. This was a woman who knew how to get what she wanted.

Daddy and Miss Bartten choreographed *West Side Story* . . . and on the side, they choreographed each other.

Mom suspected nothing, partly because Daddy was knocking himself out trying to be Super Husband. He bought Mom dazzling earrings and took her to restaurants, and told her he didn't mind at all when she had to work late . . . especially because Wall Street was forty-five minutes by train and another thirty minutes by subway, and that meant that Mom's day was twelve hours long. Dad and Miss Bartten knew exactly what to do with those long absences.

Annie sat on a window seat. How odd, thought Annie. I was sure the windows were boarded up. But none of them are.

From here, she could not see the wreckage that tenants had made of the gardens and fountains. In fact, the slashing rain had the effect of a working fountain, as if the stone nymph still threw water from her arched fingers. Rain stitched the horizon to the sea. Sean of course noticed nothing: he was a boy upon whom the world had little effect.

I want romance! she thought. But I want mine with somebody wonderful and I want Daddy's to be with Mom.

Fragmented sections of Annie glittered in the old ballroom.

Violins, decided Annie, putting the present out of her mind. And certainly a harp. A square Victorian piano. Crimson velvet on every window seat, and heavy brocade curtains with beaded fringe. I have a dance card, of course. Full, because all the young men adore me.

Annie left the window seat and danced as slowly and gracefully as she knew how. Surely in the 1890s they had done nothing but waltz, so she slid around in three-beat triangles. Her reflections danced with her.

My chaperon is sipping her punch. One of my young men is saying something naughty. I of course am blushing and looking shocked, but I say something naughty right back, and giggle behind my ivory fan.

The second falling came.

It was strong as gravity. It had a grip, and seized her ankles. She tried to kick, but it had her hands too. It had a voice, full of cruel laughter, and it had color, a bloodstained dark red.

What is happening? she thought, terrorized, but the thought was only air, and the wind that had held her hair in its fingers now possessed her thinking too. She was being turned inside out.

It was beneath her—the power was from below— taking her down. Not through the floor, but through— *through what?*

The wind screamed in circles and the mirrors split up and her grip on the world ended.

Or the world ended.

"Hey! ASL!" bellowed Sean. "Get me my metric wrenches."

But ASL did not appear.

Sean went inside. How shadowy the Mansion was, with so many windows boarded up. The place had a sick damp scent now that the tenant families had been moved out. It did not seem familiar to Sean, even though he had lived there all his life till last month. He had a weird sense that if he walked down the halls, he would not know where they went.

"Annie?" He had to swallow to get the word out.

Sean, who did not have enough imagination to be afraid of anything, and could watch any movie without being afraid, was afraid.

"Annie?" he whispered.

Nobody answered.

He went back outdoors, his hands trembling. He had to jam them into his pockets. She'd gone off without him noticing, that was all.

He couldn't concentrate on the cars. Couldn't get comfortable with his bare back exposed to the sightless, dying Mansion.

He threw his tools in the back of his MG and took off.

Annie's bike lay in the grass, wet and gleaming from the storm.

CHAPTER 2

Strat had been thinking of lemonade. He ambled toward the pullcord to summon a kitchen maid and looked through a ghost.

His dry throat grew a little drier.

Of course the heir to the Stratton fortune was also heir to a practical streak, and did not believe in ghosts. So it wasn't one.

Still, the sweat from the baseball game turned as cold as if he'd sat in the ice wagon. The white cotton shirt stuck to his chest, and Strat was sorry he'd tossed the baseball bat into the sports box in the cloakroom. He wouldn't have minded having something to swing.

Not only did the ghost approach Strat, it actually passed through him. He held very still, wanting to know how ghosts felt. Were they mist or flesh? Dampness or cloud?

Real hair, long shivery satin hair, slid over his fingers. His shudder penetrated the ghost, which reached with half-present hands to feel him. Its touch missed, reaching instead an old Greek statue in the wall niche. It stroked the fine white marble and then fingered the fresh flowers wreathed around it.

Strat decided against blinking. A blink was time enough for a ghost to vanish. He tried to breathe without sound and walk without vibration. The ghost moved slowly, fondling every surface. In fact, it acted like a plain, garden-variety thief, which just happened not to have all its body along. A ghost looking for something to steal.

Don't evaporate, thought Strat, following the shape.

It lingered over a huge cut glass bowl, whose sharp facets were prisms in the sunshaft, casting a hundred tiny rainbows on a white wall. It paused in front of a mirror panel, studying itself.

The ghost, and the ghost's reflections, became more solid. More vivid. And more female.

Strat was present at her birth.

The fall ended as swiftly and completely as had the first.

Out of breath and shaky, Annie struggled for balance. The wind was gone, but her heart still raced. The ballroom was strangely bright and shiny.

And full.

She was in an empty room, she could see how empty it was, and yet it was full. She had to take care

16

not to bump into people. Even the air was different: it was like breathing in flowers, so heavy was the scent.

And then—clearly—sweetly—

—she heard a harp. A violin. And a piano.

I did fall, thought Annie. Over the edge into insanity. Quick, walk outdoors. Check the oil stains on Sean's fingers. See how he steps right in the puddles without noticing his feet are wet. Listen to him tell me to fetch and carry.

But she did not go outdoors.

She went deeper and deeper into the condemned and collapsing rooms of the Mansion. As the sky turned violet from the passing storm, so did the Mansion turn violet, and then crimson, and gold. It filled with velvet and silk. It filled with sound and music. It filled with years gone by.

Annie Lockwood had fallen indeed.

She tried to think clearly, but nothing had clarity. Some strange difference in the world filled her eyes like snow and her ears like water. She couldn't see where she was putting her feet; couldn't see even the things she knew she saw.

The Mansion was changing beneath her feet, shifting under her fingertips. The world's molecules had separated. She was seeing fractions. Had she fallen into prehistory? Before the shape of things?

She had never known fear. She knew it now.

And then, beneath her own fingers, shape began.

The old walls, where paint had been layered on paint in a dozen ugly shades, turned into rich wallpaper that felt like velvet. Floors lost their splinters and grew fabulous carpets of indigo blue and Pompeii red. Ceilings lost their sag and were covered with gold leaf Greek-key designs.

She began seeing people. Half people. Not ghosts; just people who had not entirely arrived. Unless, of course, it was she, Annie, who had not entirely arrived.

I'm not real, she thought. The Mansion became real, while I, Annie Lockwood, no longer exist.

In the great front hall whose chessboard floor had always seemed such a reflection of cruelty, she looked up through banisters heavy with monsters. Etched glass, like lace printed on the windows, dripped with sungold. Twelve-foot-high armloads of heavy suffocating fabric fell from the sides of each window and crept across the floor. The staircase was both beauty and threat.

Whatever she was, she still possessed sight. She had to turn her eyes away from the glare. She could half focus now, and in the shadows beneath the great stair was something dark and narrow. Half seen, or perhaps only half there, were half people. But they were full of emotion, and the emotion was Fury.

Fury like a painting. There was fighting. Hissing and clenched fists and fierce words. How black it was, compared to the glittering sunshaft! Black that slithered with its own sound. Smoke like apples and autumn filled the air.

And then somebody fell. It was like her own fall getting here: steep and jagged and forever. The sound of breaking bones was new to Annie's ears, but there was no doubt what had happened. A skull had cracked like glass in that dark space.

Annie whirled to get out of there. Around her, the walls became heavier and more real.

I'm in the Mansion, she thought, but it feels like a tomb. Am I locked in here like a pharaoh's bride with all my furniture and servants?

She patted surfaces, trying to find the way out, as if there were some little door somewhere, some tiny staircase up to . . .

To what?

What was happening?

A dining room now. Real cherry wood. Real damask. Real pale pink roses in a real china vase.

The fury and the blackness and the smoke froze halfway into her mind, like history half studied.

What had she seen on the stairs? A real murder?

I don't need a real murder, thought Annie Lockwood. I need a real way out.

She waded through half-there rooms, reaching, touching, making wishes—and bumped into somebody.

Strat followed her, hypnotized. She wore a white dress, rather short, several inches above her ankles. She wore no gloves. She had no hat. Although it was midafternoon, her hair was down.

In the evening, when his mother back in Brooklyn Heights was preparing for bed, she would take down her hair. When he was a little boy, Strat had loved that, how the long U-shaped pins released that knot and turned Mama into a completely different, much softer person.

His ghost was continuously becoming a different softer person. Strat gasped. *The girl's legs were bare.*

But she was almost his own height! This was no eight-year-old. Bare legs! Perhaps it's a new sort of tennis costume, he thought, hoping that indeed tennis costumes were going to feature bare-legged girls from now on.

They had installed a tennis court on the estate, and Strat was quite taken by the game. When he began Yale next year he intended to go out for baseball and crew and tennis. Strat did not see how he was going to do all the necessary sports and still attend class.

Harriett and Devonny adored tennis and played it often, but Strat could not imagine either girl without white stockings to cover her limbs.

His sister, Devonny, had no chaperon to chastise her for unbecoming behavior. Father, Mother and even Florinda thought anything Devonny did was becoming. Devonny might actually take up the bare-legged style.

Harriett, however, had a so-called aunt, a second cousin who'd never married, poor worthless creature, and Aunt Ada was now Harriett's chaperon, eternally present to stop Harriett from enjoying anything ever.

Strat understood why Harriett wanted to marry young and get away from Aunt Ada, but Strat, although he loved Harriett, was not willing to marry young or even ever, as it did not seem to be a very desirable position.

Certainly neither his father nor his mother nor any of his three stepmothers had found marriage pleasant.

Devonny argued that all these women had been married to Father, and who could ever be happy under those circumstances? Whereas Harriett would be married to Strat, and therefore live happily ever after.

Strat was about as certain of happily ever after as he was of ghosts.

The ghost ahead of him touched everything. She ran her fingers over banisters and newel posts, over statuary and brass knobs and the long gold-fringed knots that cascaded from the rims of the wine-dark draperies.

Strat didn't risk speech. He simply followed her. In spite of the fact that the house was occupied by a large staff, plenty of family and several houseguests, the ghost seemed to feel comfortably alone.

She passed through the library, the morning room and the orangerie where Florinda's plants gasped for breath in the summer heat. Then she turned and headed straight for him. Strat stood very still, looking right through her, which was so strange, so impossible, and once more she bumped into him.

She didn't quite see him, and yet she said, *Oh, I'm so sorry.* Her voice was not quite there. Her lips moved, but the sound was far away, like bells on a distant island.

Even though he couldn't quite see her, he could judge that she was beautiful—and puzzled. There was

21

a faint frown on her lovely face, as though she, too, was trying to figure out why she was here, and what she was after.

She climbed the stairs.

Strat followed.

She touched the velvet cushions stacked on the landing's window seat. Strat's mother, who had had the house designed back before Father disposed of her, adored window seats. The house was tipsy with them. Nobody ever sat in one. They weren't the slightest bit comfortable.

The ghost girl touched the paintings on the wall. Mama adored Paris even more than window seats and had visited often, buying anything on a canvas. Father had not permitted Mama to keep a single French oil.

Now the ghost girl touched the Greek statues in the deep niches that lined the second landing. It was very fashionable, acquiring marbles from ancient civilizations. They had more back in Manhattan in the town house.

The girl proceeded to go through every bedroom.

She went into Father's bedroom, where luckily there was no Father present; Father lived in his study or on his golf course. He'd had his own nine hole course landscaped in a few years ago. It was too placid a sport for Strat, but it kept Father busy and away from his two children, and this was good.

Now she went into his stepmother Florinda's bedroom, and even into Florinda's bath. Strat stayed in the hall. Strat happened to know that Florinda was there, preparing for tonight's party, but no scream came from

Florinda, although she was a woman much given to screaming and fainting and whimpering and simpering.

Florinda didn't see her, thought Strat. I'm the only one who sees her. She's mine.

Strat loved that. He loved owning things. He loved knowing that every dog, horse, servant, bush, building and acre of this estate were—or would be—his. Now he had his own ghost.

All of her flawless. And so skimpily dressed! No corset, no camisole, no bloomers, no petticoats, no stockings, no hat. Strat yearned to imagine her without even the thin white dress, but it would not be honorable, so he prevented himself from having such a fantasy.

The girl walked into *his* bedroom.

This time Strat went along. Straight to the window she went, and that was sensible, for Strat's tower had a view all the way down the coastline to the city of New York. Strat liked to pretend he could pick out the steeples of Trinity Church, or the new thirteen story Tower Building on Broadway, but of course he really couldn't. What he could see was miles of congested water traffic on Long Island Sound: barges and steamers, scows and sailboats.

Strat's ghost gasped, stifling a cry with her hand, clenching frightened fingers on top of her mouth. She whirled, seeing the room and the furnishings, but not Strat. There were tears in her eyes. Her chin was quivering.

Strat was not fanciful. He disliked fiction, reading

23

only what he had been forced to read in boarding school. He'd dragged himself through *The Scarlet Letter* and *A Tale of Two Cities* and the latest nightmare, *Moby Dick*. Books that long should be outlawed. Strat preferred to read newspapers or science books. Actually, Strat preferred sports.

His stepmother, Florinda, and his sister, Devonny, were addicted to bad cheap novels full of hysterical females who fell in love without parental permission or saw ghosts or both. He'd never waste time on that balderdash. So it was amazing that he was imagining a half-there, beautiful girl. Strat hardly ever imagined anything.

What would it be like to kiss a girl like that? Strat had done little kissing in his life.

His experiences with girls were either in public, like the ever popular ice cream parlor, or chaperoned. Harriett, for example, was never available without Aunt Ada. This winter, Aunt Ada had come when Strat took Harriett ice skating; Aunt Ada had come when he took Harriett on a sleigh ride; Aunt Ada had come to the theater with them, and the opera.

Strat was pretty sick of Aunt Ada.

If Aunt Ada were to fall down the stairs and break her hip, Strat would eagerly find nurses to care for her, hoping Aunt Ada would spend many months, or maybe her lifetime, as an invalid.

If there was one thing that his ghost girl was not, it was chaperoned.

The girl slipped by him. He tried to catch her arm, but she ran too quickly for him, rushing down the stairs so fast and lightly she hardly touched them. Her little white shoes clicked on each gleaming tread. Mama, of course, had had carpet commissioned to cover the stairs; Florinda, of course, had had it torn up. Each stepmother seemed to feel that a gesture of ownership was required.

The girl ran out the front door, unmanned at the moment by a servant, since the staff was so busy putting together the party. Strat tore after her. His own bike was tilted up against the big stone pillars of the porte cochere, and there, astonishingly, lying on the grass, was a second bike.

Her bike.

She got on, and Strat, laughing out loud this time, got on his. She half heard him laugh, turned, and half saw him. The fear that had been half there was now complete, and had her in its grip. "It's all right," called Strat. "You're all right, don't be afraid, it's only me, I won't hurt you. Wait for me!"

She took off with amazing speed. Definitely not a girl who waited for anybody.

"Stop!" he yelled. "You're going too fast!" She was safe at that speed as long as she didn't meet horses coming up, but once she reached the bottom of the Great Hill, she'd be on gravel and the wheels would fly out from under her. He wondered if ghosts could break bones.

Strat pedaled furiously to catch up. The two of them flew down the curve and out onto the lane. Neither fell, but she had to stick both feet out to steady herself. Her skirt flared up wonderfully and he was shocked but happy.

He caught up.

They pedaled next to each other for a full minute, and then she stopped dead, so fast he nearly went over his handlebars. She balanced on her toes like a ballerina and they stared at each other.

Strat was entranced. She was his possession; his mirage; his very own beautiful half-ghost. "Good afternoon," said Strat.

"*Who* are *you?*" she said, as if greeting an exotic Red Indian.

"Hiram Stratton, Junior," he said cheerfully.

"I'm Annie Lockwood. What's going on? Everything is really strange. Like, where are the picnic grounds? Where are the parking lots? What happened to the traffic? And what on earth are you wearing?"

Strat felt that since it was his estate, he should be the one to ask questions. Irritated but courteous (a boy on stepmother number three and boarding school roommate number eleven knew how to be polite even when extremely irritated), Strat said, "I'm not sure to what you are referring, Miss Lockwood. But you just walked right through my home, room by room, when my own personal plan called for having iced lemonade."

She rewarded him with a wonderful smile, infectious and friendly. He had to smile back. Poor Harriett's teeth stuck out and overlapped. Miss Lockwood's smile was white and perfect and full of delight. *She* would never have to keep her lips closed when the photographer came. "Iced lemonade sounds wonderful," she told him. "I have had a super weird day. And I am so sweaty," she confided.

Strat was appalled. What lady would say that word? Horses might sweat, but ladies were dewy.

"What are you wearing?" she asked again, looking down at his trousers as if he were as undressed as she.

He was wearing perfectly ordinary knee-length breeches. A perfectly ordinary white shirt, with lots of room in it, was neatly tucked in in spite of the chase she had just led.

Strat considered his lemonade offer. He was not willing to take Miss Lockwood back to the house. Share her with his sister, or Harriett, or Florinda, or his father, or Aunt Ada or the staff? Never. There was no way he could possibly explain what he had just seen. The birth of a ghost? Besides, she was his. He wanted to find out who she was, and how she got here, and he wanted her to be his own personal possession.

"Let's cycle into the village," he said. "I'll take you to the ice cream parlor. We'll have a soda."

"Deal," she said unfathomably. "Do I call you Hiram? You must have a nickname. I mean, they couldn't have saddled you with the name Hiram and then called you that."

"The boys call me Strat," he said uncertainly. Girls, of course, called him Mr. Stratton. Even Harriett, whom he had known forever, and who was now his own father's ward, called him Strat only in small gatherings, and never when there were strangers around.

But the girl had no qualms about getting familiar.

"Strat," she repeated, smiling again, giving him the strangest shiver of desire. "Let's race. I'll win." She took off.

Strat could not believe this. Let's race? I'll win? Girls weren't allowed to do either one!

To his shame, it was immediately clear that Miss Lockwood might just do both. Strat took off after her and the contest was fierce. Gravel spurted from their tires. Wind picked up her long unbound hair so it flowed out behind her like some wonderful drawing. Strat stood up on the pedals and churned hard. There was no way he would tolerate a beating by a girl who hadn't even existed ten minutes ago!

But the race ended long before they reached the village, for Miss Lockwood stopped short, staring at the gatehouse.

Brown-shingled, intricately turreted, it was a miniature of the Mansion. Its long arm crossed the lane to prevent unwanted carriages from entering. The gatekeeper smiled from the watch window. "Good afternoon, sir."

Strat waved.

"What is this?" said Miss Lockwood. She was so frightened she was angry.

"The gatehouse," he said soothingly. "You must have passed it on your way in." But she didn't come by bike, he thought, nor by carriage, nor by boat. I saw her. She came by . . .

Strat had no idea how she had come, only that he had been there when it happened. Where had her bike come from? He had witnessed her arrival and there

28

had been no bike. He did not exactly feel fear, but rather a confusion so deep he didn't want to get near the edge of it.

"There is no building like this," she said, her voice getting high. "And that field. And that meadow. *Where are the houses?*"

"The land's been sold for building," agreed Strat. He tried to keep his voice level and comforting, the way he did with Florinda during fainting fits. "It's become fashionable to build by the water. Two or three years, and we'll have neighbors here."

She really stared at him now. It was unladylike, her degree of concentration on him. "Strat, who are you?" Her voice wasn't ladylike either; it demanded an answer.

It unsettled him to be called Strat by a person who had known him only moments. "I think a more interesting point is who you are, Miss Lockwood. And where you came from. When I followed you, as you trespassed in my house, you were—" He couldn't say it. Half there? Nonsense. It was too foolish. Too female.

"When I felt the cushions and the drapes, I couldn't believe it," she said. "They were real and I was there. Velvet and silk."

Strat wanted to touch her velvet cheek, and stroke her silken hair. He had never wanted to touch anything so much.

Am I just curious to see if she's real, he thought, or is this love?

He desperately wanted to find out what love was.

29

Things with Harriett were so settled and ordinary. Strat wanted something breathless and wonderful.

Perhaps I shall fall in love with Miss Lockwood, he thought. True love, not just being attentive to Harriett.

His sister, Devonny, was an expert in affairs of the heart, but Devonny said Strat did not get to participate, as he simply belonged to Harriett and that was his only heart possibility.

One more look at Miss Lockwood and Strat wanted her as his heart possibility. "Let's leave the bikes here, Miss Lockwood," he said, fighting for breath as if she had pulled him underwater. "Let's walk on the sand."

And she said "Yes," taking his hand as if they had known each other for years.

Harriett and Devonny went through the sheet music, planning what each girl would play on the piano for the singing that night. Harriett and Devonny had very different tastes. Harriett liked sad ballads where everybody died by verse six and on verse seven you wept for them. Devonny liked madcap dances where you couldn't get the words out fast enough to match the chords she played.

Harriett did not tell Devonny how upset she was. It was very important, when you were a lady, to hide emotions and maintain a calm and dignified face. If you were to frown and glare and grimace, your complexion would be ruined and you would get wrinkles early.

But Strat, she had clearly seen from the window,

had gone cycling with some girl in a white sports costume. How much easier tennis would be in an outfit that short. But it was unthinkable to display your limbs like that. Harriett could not imagine who the girl might be.

It couldn't be a servant; Harriett knew all of them; and they would be let go immediately were they to dress so improperly or even for a moment to entertain a thought of romance with young Mr. Stratton.

Of course you read novels in which the Irish serving girl fell in love with the millionaire's son and they ran off together, and Harriett loved that sort of book, but in real life it was not acceptable. Especially *her* real life. And the Irish serving girl they had, Bridget, was even now holding the parasol for Florinda's stroll through the garden, so it was not Bridget out there with Strat.

Harriett did not usually like to face the beveled mirrors that were omnipresent in the ballroom, but she forced herself. Harriett was plain and her teeth stuck out. She was two years older than Strat. She did not have a wasp waist like Devonny. No matter how tightly Bridget yanked the corset, Harriett remained solid. Her hair was on the thin side, and did not take well to the new fashions. She had always expected to pin false ringlets into her hair where necessary. But of course she had to reach womanhood when the style became simpler, and women fluffed their hair on top of their heads, plumping it out like Gibson girls. Harriett's hair neither plumped nor fluffed.

Sweet Strat always complimented her anyway.

How lovely you look, he would say. How glad I am to see you, Harriett.

And he was glad to see her, and he did spend many hours with her, and he even put up with Aunt Ada.

But underneath, Harriett was always afraid. What if she did not get married? Of course, with her wealth, she would find some husband, somewhere. But she did not want some husband somewhere. She wanted Strat, here.

The mirrors cut her into fragments and multiplied her throughout the ballroom. Wherever she turned, she saw how plain and dull she was. Don't cry, she reminded herself. Don't slouch.

These were the rules Aunt Ada gave Harriett, when what Harriett yearned for was love.

Devonny would have reported in to Harriett if Strat had ever said he was thinking of another girl. The family assumed that Strat and Harriett would wed, but the fact remained that Strat had never, by the slightest syllable, suggested such a thing.

And he was eighteen now, and she twenty.

He should, by now, have suggested such a thing.

She did not want him going to Yale. All those other young men would have sisters. Beautiful sisters, no doubt. And each needing a railroad baron's son in wedlock. Strat would go to parties without Harriett, and be dazzled by beauties especially prepared to snag him. And one of them might—for the rich and beautiful chose each other, and Harriett, although richest of all, was plain.

She wished they didn't use that word wedlock. It sounded very locked up and very locked in.

Unless you were Strat's father, of course, who unlocked every marriage as soon as he arrived in it. He was the only man Harriett had ever met who had actually had a divorce, and he had had three of them. Would son be like father? Would she be sorry, wedlocked to Strat?

Pretending an errand, Harriett left Devonny at the piano and ran up the great staircase and down the guest wing, praying no houseguest would hear her footsteps and join her. The highest tower had its own narrow twist of steps, and the fullness of her skirts made climbing it difficult. The tower had two window seats (the influence of the first Mrs. Stratton reached everywhere) and also a tiny desk, a telescope for viewing ships and birds and stars, and beautifully bound blank journals for making entries about those birds and stars. Apparently nobody was all that fascinated by natural history because the journals remained blank.

At the top she could turn in a circle and see the entire island.

Mr. Stratton senior, of course, had built a causeway linking the island to the village, but Harriett still thought of it as an island, because when she was a little girl, it could be reached only at low tide, ladies lifting their skirts in a most unseemly way, and children darting among the horseshoe crabs.

There, on the long white stretch of sand, where fragrant beach grass stopped and tidal debris began, walked Strat and the unknown girl . . . arm in arm.

Be ladylike, Harriett said to herself. Do not spy on your dearest friend. Take this calmly and return to the piano.

She focused the telescope. It displayed Strat and his beautiful stranger sitting together in the sand. After a bit they crawled forward to where the sand was still wet from the tide, to build a castle. The girl kicked off her shoes and was barefoot in the sand.

I will not cry, said Harriett to herself. I will not let him know that I saw. I will not ask. I will mind my manners.

She burst into tears anyway. I will so ask! Who does he think he is! He can't—

But he could, of course.

It was his estate, and the barefoot girl was his guest, and he was not affianced to Harriett, and he had all the rights, and Harriett had none.

"What are you doing up here?" said Devonny. "Goodness, Harriett, you're all puffy-eyed! What's the matter?" Devonny searched the view and immediately saw what was the matter.

"Harriett!" she shrieked. "Who is that girl? Look what they're doing! Harriett, what *are* they doing? I've never seen anybody do that! Harriett, who is she?"

She is, thought Harriett, the end of my hopes.

CHAPTER 3

Annie had no pockets, but Strat's were deep and saggy, so she filled them with beach treasure—mermaids' tears. Sand-smoothed broken glass brought in by the tide. When she slipped her hand into his pocket, Strat tensed as if she were doing something daring, and then let out his breath as if she were the treat of a lifetime. He looked at her the way Annie had always dreamed a boy would look at her: as if she were a work of art, the best one in the world.

Strat's hair was blunt cut in an unfamiliar way. Longish, somehow, even though lots of boys Annie knew wore their hair much longer. His shirt collar was open, the collar itself larger than collars should be. His pants were high-waisted, instead of slung down toward the hips, and his suspenders were real, actually holding the pants up, instead of decorating his shirt.

Annie concentrated on details, because the large

event was beyond thought. If she began adding things up, she would get a very strange number, a number she did not want to have. Yet she certainly wanted to have Strat. "Strat," she repeated. It suited him. He was both jock and preppie, both formal and informal.

He arranged her hand lightly on his forearm, joining himself to her in a distant, well-mannered way. Down the sand they walked.

The beach wasn't right. There were dunes. The beach Annie knew had been flattened by a million bare feet. Here, the tide line was littered with driftwood from shipwrecks and mounds of oyster shells, as if no beach crew raked and no day campers collected treasure.

Nobody was there except Annie and the boy from the Mansion.

Nobody.

Even on the most frigid bleak day in January, Stratton Point wouldn't be empty. You'd have your photography nut, your birding group, your idiot who plunged into the water all twelve months of the year, your joggers and miscellaneous appreciators of nature.

Absolutely nobody else was on the half mile of white sand. In spite of the heat, Annie trembled.

"Miss Lockwood," Strat began.

She loved the Miss Lockwood stuff. It took away the shivers and made her giggle.

There was a courtliness to Strat that she'd never seen in a man or a boy. He was treating her like a fragile dried rose. A contrast to Sean, who often told

36

(not asked) her to throw his toolbox in the back of the truck for him.

The sun caught her eyes, blinding her for a moment, and she pulled back her hair to see him better. His features were heavier than Sean's, firmer, somehow more demanding.

"Please forgive me any rudeness, Miss Lockwood, but I am unsure . . ." His voice trailed off, his mouth slightly open, waiting for a really good phrase. His nose was sunburned.

He is so handsome, thought Annie. If I'd ever seen him before in my life, I would certainly remember. And I would remember the gatehouse, if it existed. What happened here? Who is he? And who am I?

"I was there when you arrived," he said finally. "And I am unsure about what I saw."

The only possibility was too ridiculous to say out loud. *I fell down, Strat, and I think the fall was not between standing and sitting. I think it was between centuries.*

Right.

"I'm pretty unsure myself, Strat," she said. "What *is* going on? Do *you* know? I've lost track of some time here. Maybe a whole lot of time. Don't laugh at me."

"I would not dream of laughing, Miss Lockwood," he promised, and now his features were earnest, worried and respectful.

Annie tried to imagine any boy on the football team or in the cafeteria talking as courteously as Strat. They'd be more apt to swear as they demanded information.

Far to the east, the thunderstorm quickstepped out to the ocean, black clouds roiling over black clouds. Above Strat and Annie, the sky turned lavender blue, not a single remaining wisp of cloud.

It's a dream, she thought. I'm having an electric storm of the mind, just as the sky had its electrical storm. Little flashes of story are sparking through. Nothing makes sense in dreams, so I don't have to worry about sense.

But she had senses, the other kind, in this dream: touch and feel, smell and taste. The smell, especially, of a beach at low tide. Hot summery salt and seaweed. You did not carry smell into your dreams. "I know we're at Stratton Point," she said carefully.

He raised his eyebrows. He looked wicked for a moment, capable of anything, and then he grinned again and looked capable mainly of being adorable. "I'm a Stratton," he said, "but we call the estate Llanmarwick."

"I've lived in the village all my life, and I've never heard anybody use that word."

"Well, we certainly get our supplies delivered. Llanmarwick with two l's," said Strat cheerfully. "Mama got it from a novel about Wales. I do believe it's a fake word. Of course Florinda would like to change it. She wants to call it Sea Mere, but Devonny and I are fighting to keep Llanmarwick."

Annie felt no shyness, the way she normally would with a strange boy, or even a very well-known boy, because so little was normal here. "Let's sit," she whispered, pulling him down beside her in the hot comforting sand. Were his cute little knickers really corduroy? Could she feel him? Or like the half-there furnishings of the Mansion, was he insubstantial? She explored him with an interest she had never felt for Sean, and Strat turned out to be substantial indeed.

His skin was real. His sunburn, tan and freckles were real. His eyebrows barely separated and she threaded a finger down his nose and back up between his brows. He seemed to feel he had been given permission by her touch to do the same, and her movements were mirrored. Whatever she did, he reflected back.

Mirrors, she thought, caught on a sharp fragment of knowledge. What is it about mirrors that I should remember?

"Shouldn't you be wearing your hat?" he said abruptly. It was one of those sentences to fill space, when you don't want to talk at all, but you don't know what else to do.

You are so lovable, she thought, you're like a teddy bear dressed in sweet old-fashioned clothes. "I would never wear a hat. Maybe if I took up skiing, I'd jam some knitted thing over my ears, but that's just a good reason not to ski. I hate flattening my hair."

"You never wear a hat?" He was unable to believe this.

Their eyes met on the subject of hats, of all things. Well, she had wanted a conversation that went beyond machines and cars, and she had it.

He was wearing a hat: a flat, beretlike cap with a little brim, the sort men wore in movies about early cars with running boards. It was gray plaid and cute. She took his hat off, taking time to run her fingers through his heavy hair, as if she, having met Strat, now owned him. She put his cap on her own head and gave him a teasing half-smile. "There. Fully hatted," she said. "Better?"

Then there were no facts and no time span, only sense. Touch and feel and smell and sight: these four as perfect as dreams. It is a dream, she thought. Real life isn't this wonderful.

So if it's a dream, there is nothing to do but sleep it out, enjoy whatever comes, because when I awaken—

A sound Annie had never heard in real life, only on television, filled her ears. A heavy metal striking; a thudding clippy-clop, clippy-clop.

Annie leaped to her feet. There, beyond the bayberry bushes and the sea grass and the dunes, were four beautiful horses, rich ruddy brown with braided manes, grandly pulling a carriage decorated like a Christmas tree, with golden scrollwork: the Stratton initials. The guard in the little gatehouse had lifted the gate, and the carriage passed onto Stratton Point without missing a beat.

Annie filled with time.

Filled with fear.

No.

There is no such thing as falling through time.

Without her permission, the facts added themselves up. The view from the bedroom tower, from which there had been no interstate bridge across the river. The wild empty beach. This boy, with his oddly cut hair, manners, clothing. That carriage.

No.

They're filming an historical movie, she informed herself. Somebody paid a trillion dollars to take down the phone poles and lay turf over the parking lots and close off the beach. Somehow on the last day of school, nobody talked about this, although obviously the entire village is cooperating to the fullest.

The horses snorted, and stamped, the rich aroma of their sweat masking the scent of the sea. Annie forced herself to look way up the beach and over the clear meadow to the old stables. *They were not old.* They were new. The doors had not been taken off so that tractors and trucks could fit through. Horses lived in that stable.

"Strat?" she whispered. The ocean roared in her ears, although there were no waves to speak of; the day was calm. It's fear roaring in my ears, she thought. "What year is this, Strat?"

"Miss Lockwood, it is 1895."

She felt as if she would fall again, and she clung to him. It was a circumstance with which he was familiar—fainting women—and he responded much more comfortably than to the bike race. The carriage moved on, while Annie remained within his arms. "This really is 1895?" said Annie.

"It really is."

She had half fallen to the ground. He'd knelt to catch her, and now she was sitting on his bent knee,

Strat staring at her like a man about to propose. "We have a problem," said Annie. "I live in 1995."

"I'm good at guessing games," he said. "I'll have this in a moment. Is that a clue to your street address?"

But Annie Lockwood had finished her own guessing game and was pretty sure of the truth. She tucked his arm tighter around herself, as if she were an infant to be comforted by wrapped blankets. Eighteen ninety-five. Not only is this boy really a Stratton, she thought, my parents aren't even born yet—my grandparents aren't born yet! "I'm sorry I dizzied out on you, Strat. I just caught on, that's all. I really am in 1895. I've fallen backward a century. Which can't happen. I have to figure out what has gone wrong, Strat."

"Sun," said Strat with certainty. "Young ladies are never allowed out in the sun without hats, and this is why. Your constitution isn't strong enough. Young ladies are too frail for the heat. We'll go home and you'll rest on Florinda's fainting couch."

She saw that he did not want to accept the century change at all, and would far rather have some un-chaperoned girl who needed to rest on a fainting couch. Who was Florinda, and why did she faint so often that she needed a special couch on which to do it?

"No, Strat, you were there. You're the one I bumped into, aren't you? You saw half of me when I saw half of you. It isn't too much sun, Strat."

Fragments like triangular photographs, caught in the mirrors of the Mansion, flickered in Annie's memory. She saw again the blackness shifting, smelled the apples and autumn, heard the crack of bone.

What did I see? she thought. Did I see it in this time, or as I fell through? I remember the blackness had its own sound. But that is as impossible as changing centuries.

Strat's face shifted too, becoming young and upset. "I was there," he admitted. "And you're right, it wasn't sun. We were indoors, you and I, and most of the drapes were pulled to keep out the sun. I don't know why I said that. I'm sorry."

They touched but not as they had before: they touched to see if the other was real, if the skin was alive and the cheek was warm.

"I've fallen through time. I'm from a hundred years later, Strat." She had no watch. The sky was a late-afternoon sky. A four or five o'clock sky.

"Was it frightening?" said Strat.

"Yes. It was really a fall. I could feel the time rushing past my face. There were other people in there with me. Half people." I'm not the only one changing centuries, thought Annie. Other bodies and souls flew past me. Or with me. Or through me.

"Are you frightened now?" said Strat, discarding the scary parts and eager to move on into the adventure. "Don't be. I'll take care of you. You'll stay with us. We'll have to come up with a story, though. We can't use time travel. It's too bad Devonny isn't here, she's wonderful at fibs."

Stay with him? thought Annie, touching the idea the way she had touched Strat's face. Stay in the Mansion, he means! I'd have my wish. I'd see how they live, and wear their dresses, and dance their dances! I'd have both lives. Both centuries.

The last time she'd had that thought, she had also thought of Daddy having both women. Now the knowledge of Daddy's affair traveled with her over the century and ruined the adventure. She shook her head. "I have to get home, Strat. How will I get home? I don't know how I got here, never mind how to go in the other direction. I should go right now, before they worry. Mom will have left a message on the machine asking about the last half day."

Strat had no idea what that meant.

"Of course, Mom isn't home from work yet," added Annie, "which means that so far nobody's worried."

"Your mother works?" said Strat, horrified.

"Well, she doesn't swab prison toilets," said Annie, laughing at him. "She works on Wall Street."

"Your mother?"

"She's a very successful account executive."

Annie envisioned her mother, with that distinguished wardrobe, black or gray or ivory or olive, always formal, always businesslike. That briefcase, bulging, and that Powerbook, charged, as indeed Mom was charged every day, eager to get to New York and get to work. Annie thought her mother very beautiful, but Daddy had changed his mind on the definition of beauty.

What if I can't get back to her? thought Annie. She'll need me and I won't be there! How could the universe let me fall through like that? Why didn't I go through the first time I fell? What made it happen the second time? How can I find the way back out? Is it a door? A wish? A magic stone?

Strat led her up the sloping sand to the causeway as gently as if he were comforting a grieving widow. Now he was actually lifting her bike for her, quite obviously preparing to help her get on. Could any girl on earth require help to get on her bike? He was being so gentle with her she felt like a newborn kitten, or a woman who used fainting couches. How maddening.

"My constitution," said Annie Lockwood, "just happens to be superlative. Especially in the sun. I can whip you at beach volleyball any day of the week, fella. As for tennis, you'll be begging for mercy. Bet I can swim farther than you too."

"What is volleyball?" he asked. "I do play tennis, though, and I'm perfectly willing to beg for mercy. But if you are so hale and hearty that you can whip me, then let us forget fainting couches. May I have the honor of escorting you to the village to the ice cream parlor, Miss Lockwood?"

He was not being sarcastic. He was not being silly. He was actually hoping for the honor.

Nobody says things like that, thought Annie. Not out loud. You'd be laughed out of school. Laughed off the team.

"Before you change centuries again, of course," added Strat.

It didn't matter what century you saw that grin in. He had a world-class grin. Annie decided to worry about changing centuries after ice cream.

They mounted their bikes.

He stared at how much of her leg was revealed until she adjusted the white skirt to cover her thigh. All this attention was delightful. Sean wouldn't have noticed if she'd danced on the ceiling.

"Let's not race," said Strat. "Let's pedal slowly."

Let's keep that skirt in place, translated Annie. "Okay," she said.

"If we run into my friends," said Strat, as they moved down a road that was not paved, but graded and oiled, "I'll introduce you, of course. May I know your real name? Annie must be what your family calls you."

I do have a real name, thought Annie. And what's more, a *perfect* real name. Perhaps I was meant to fall through. Perhaps it was intended that I should visit another era, and my parents had no choice but to give me the name of another era. "Anna Sophia," she said. It was supposed to happen. I must stop worrying about getting back. Everything will happen at the right time, just as I must have fallen through at the right time.

She was wildly exhilarated now, unworried, ready to have a huge crush on this sweet boy.

He claimed to love Anna Sophia as a name, but continued to call her Miss Lockwood.

They pedaled a quarter mile.

Miss Lockwood held her hand out to Mr. Stratton, and he took it in his, and they pedaled hand in hand, and did not worry about traffic, because there was no such thing.

*　　*　　*

Bridget, the little Irish maid, loved parties as much as Miss Devonny and Miss Harriett. Of course, she didn't get to dance, but she got to look. She would help the ladies dress, and help with the ladies' hair, and for a moment or two could actually hold the diamond brooch or the strings of pearls.

She'd been up since before the sun, and would not be permitted rest until the party ended and the ladies were abed. She wasn't tired. Bridget was used to work.

She'd left her family in Ireland only three years ago, when she was thirteen years old, walking country lanes until she reached the Atlantic, and crossing that terrible ocean in the bottom of an even more terrible boat, and she had been hungry all those thirteen years but she was not hungry now.

She'd done the right thing, coming to America. It tickled Bridget that she was taking care of a fourteen-year-old, Miss Devonny, who was not even allowed to cross a street by herself, while she, Bridget, had crossed an ocean. Bridget enjoyed life, and she certainly enjoyed the Mansion. The party tonight would be magnificent, things undreamed of in all Ireland. And although she couldn't dance at the dance, she nevertheless had a dance partner.

She was stepping out with the grocery delivery boy. Of course Jeb's parents, staunch Congregationalists, were horrified that their son was in love with a Catholic. They were going to send him out West, or enlist him in the army—anything to get him out of the

47

vile clutches of Bridget Shanrahan. So her romance with Jeb was more romantic than anything Miss Devonny or Miss Harriett would ever have—clandestine meetings, dark corners, plotting against parents, and the true and valid fear that they would never be permitted to marry.

Bridget polished. She polished silver, she polished brass, she polished copper, she polished wood. The Mansion gleamed wherever Bridget had been, and in the beautiful wood of the piano Bridget looked at her reflection and hoped that her clutches were not vile, but also hoped they were strong enough to work.

I have gotten what I wanted so far. The thing is not to give up. My sisters and brothers gave up, and they're still back there, starving and hopeless.

Tears fell onto the perfect piano and she swiftly soaked up the evidence. Weakness was very pretty in a lady like Miss Florinda. But Bridget had not had the luck to be born a lady. Weakness would destroy her. She prayed to Our Lady for help. *Please let Jeb stand up to his family and love me most!*

Harriett could tell by the way Strat tossed back his head and faced the girl sitting on his knee that he was having a wonderful time. I have never sat on his knee, she thought. I have never sat on any man's knee. No man has held my face in his hands like that.

Her heart blistered. Her hands turned thick and heavy like rubber, while the hands of that girl on the beach were touching Strat in ways Harriett had never thought of, never mind dared.

"Well!" said Devonny. "We have to nip this in the bud! You and I have planned the most magnificent wedding in America for you and Strat. Photographers will come from Europe. We'll all go on the honeymoon with you. It won't be any fun if Strat marries somebody else, Harriett."

"I don't know that he's proposing marriage to her," said Harriett, as mildly as she knew how. Her heart was not feeling mild. She was using up all the control she possessed at this moment, and when Strat came back—with this girl?—she would have no self-control left. She would be stripped down to the heart and do something crazed and stupid.

"He'll have to marry her if he keeps that up," said Devonny.

Harriett knew slightly more about the facts of life than Devonny. Strat was not compromising the unknown girl's future. Not yet.

"I still say I want your honeymoon in the Wild West," said Devonny, as if Harriett had been protesting.

Devonny never planned her own wedding and honeymoon, only her brother's to Harriett. It was the thing now to take your entire wedding party to Yellowstone. There was a fine new lodge, built by Union Pacific Railroad. The party would frolic for a few weeks at those geysers, and see a grizzly bear, and then go on to the Pacific Ocean. Perhaps a few weeks in that little town of San Francisco would be pleasant. They would wander in the hills and find gold.

Strat was gold enough. If only Harriett could have Strat—if only she could become his wife! The horror of being a spinster gripped Harriett by the spine, as if not being married could paralyze her.

When Strat came back for the party this evening, would he bring this girl? Would he introduce her? Would he say, This is Miss Somebody, with whom I have fallen in love? Would he expect Harriett to be friendly to her?

Of course he would. He always expected the best of Harriett.

"Strat wandered," said Devonny, using the verb to mean unfaithful. "He's going to do that, you know. He will be like Father. You must put up with it, Harriett, even after you're married."

They were very sheltered young ladies, but they knew the truth about fathers. Harriet's father had had mistresses, strings of them, and her mother had not been allowed to mind. Of course, Mother had died young of tuberculosis, sparing Harriett's father the trouble of worrying about his wife's feelings. Harriett's father then died, thrown from his horse in a silly pointless race. Harriett missed her father dreadfully. She knew, in a distant sort of way, that she wanted Strat to be her father as well as her husband, and she knew, less distantly, that there was something wrong with that. But if only she could be married to him, then everything would be all right, and the gaping holes where she was not loved would be filled.

Devonny's father was also a gaping hole of loveless-ness. He would certainly not be missed were he to meet with an accident. He was completely sinful, divorcing his wives and getting new ones. Divorce was unthinkable, except in Devonny's family, where it was thought of quite routinely. Strat and Devonny's mother had been placed in a town house in Brooklyn, and hadn't been given enough money to leave.

Harriet hoped Strat had more of his mother in him than his father. Mr. Stratton senior was a rude cruel man who drove himself through life like a splinter through a palm. But Strat was sweet and kind. On Strat, beautiful manners sat easily, and Harriet had never known him to be anything but nice.

Be nice to me, Strat, she prayed. Let me have what I want. You.

Her eyes forced her to look down the white line of sand to where it narrowed at the causeway.

The girl climbed on her cycle, and Strat mounted his, and they cycled away, laughing and talking, and the girl's hair and skirt flew out behind her like a child's, yet romantic as a woman's.

Aunt Ada had worn nothing but black for decades. In the evening, her black dress was silk, dripping with jet beads, and cascading with tied fringe. Even the shawls that kept her narrow shoulders warm were black. It was a true reflection of her life. Not one ray of light existed for her. She'd been scowling for so many years that even her smiles were downward, though very little made Ada smile.

The woman who did not marry ceased to have value, and Ada's value had ended long, long ago. The woman who did not marry had to beg, and Ada had begged from Hiram Stratton a place in his home, and been assigned the task of chaperoning Harriett.

He paid Ada nothing.

She had a room with a bath; she had clothing suitable for her station; she had a place in the family railcar and on the family yacht and at the family table. Last place.

But Ada had no money. Quite literally, Ada had not one penny. Not one silver dollar. Even the Irish maid earned money. Not once in her adult life—which was a long one—had Ada been able to make a purchase without groveling and begging for permission.

A few months ago, Ada had overheard a conversation between Devonny and Harriett. "The minute you're wed to my brother," said Devonny, "you must get rid of Aunt Ada."

"Oh, of course," said Harriett. "Can you imagine spending my entire life with that old hag marching at my heels?"

Ada was a hag, and she knew it. She was forced to know it by the mirrors that covered the walls as sheets cover beds. Wife number one had put up those mirrors, and wives two through four were so vain and so fond of their reflections that they had not taken them down. Little triangular sections of primping females—

or females too ugly to bother, like Ada—reflected a thousand times in each great room.

Get rid of me? thought Ada. And where would I go then?

The village had a poorhouse, of course. A farm to which the failures of society were sent, Ada supposed, to plant and dig turnips.

I may have become an old hag, Harriett Ranleigh, but I am not a fool, and if you are going to get rid of me when you marry young Mr. Stratton, then the first thing I will do is prevent the marriage. The second thing I will do is acquire enough money to be safe without you, Harriett Ranleigh.

Ada rubbed her hands together. They were cold dry hands.

She was a cold dry woman. In her youth, she had tried to be warm and affectionate, like other girls. But it had not worked for her, and no man had asked for such a hand in marriage. In middle age, Ada tried to make friends of neighbors and relatives. This failed. When Mr. Stratton had asked her to supervise his motherless ward, Harriett, Ada had thought she might love this little girl. But she had not grown to love Harriett, and as the years went by, Ada realized that she did not know how to love anybody.

This knowledge no longer caused her grief. She no longer wept at night. She simply became more angry, more dry, and more cold.

She usually wore gloves, as much to keep her hands warm as to be fashionable. The fingernails were yellow and ridged and looked like weapons.

Today, thinking of Harriett, whom she hated and feared, Ada raked them suddenly through the air, as if ripping the skin off Harriett's face. Across the room Ada saw shock on the face of the little Irish maid.

"Get out," said Ada, glaring. Ada despised the Irish. The country should never have let them in. It was disgusting, the way immigrants from all those worthless countries were just sailing up and strolling onto dry land. They were even commemorating immigrants now, as if it were a good thing! That ridiculous new Statue of Liberty the young people insisted they had to see! Disgraceful.

She tucked her shawl tightly against the high-collared moiré dress, and the fabrics rasped like her thoughts. You cannot waste time being fearful, Ada ordered herself. You must channel your energy into being strong and hard. There is nobody who cares about you. Nobody. You must do all the caring yourself. And if damage is done while you are taking care, remember that men do damage all the time, and never even notice.

Ada smiled suddenly, and it was good that little Bridget was not there to see the smile. The lowering ends of Ada's thin lips were full of fear and rage.

And full of plans for Harriett.

CHAPTER 4

Walker Walkley liked the finer things in life. He did not have enough of them, but if he planned right, he could acquire enough. Throughout boarding school Walk had cultivated Strat. Strat liked company, and did not understand what this friendship cost him, either in money or in pretense.

Walk had managed to live like Strat, and off Strat, for four wonderful years, and now he was going on to Yale with Strat, but it might not be that easy to sponge at college. Walk needed certainty, and he had pretty well decided on Strat's sister, Devonny.

Strat would be delighted. And Devonny, handily, was much too young for marriage, so Walk would become affianced to Devonny, and have all the family privileges, but he could postpone actually bothering with Devonny for years.

Strat would be spending July at Walk's lodge in the

Adirondacks. It was run-down and primitive now, the twelve bedrooms in desperate need of refurbishing, the immense screened veranda over the lake in worse need of repair and paint, but Strat never noticed these things, and if he did, would assume that hunting lodges were supposed to look like that. Musty old stuffed moose heads on the wall and rotting timber in the floor.

Walk worried about discussing the finances with Mr. Stratton senior, who was a tough and hostile man under the best of circumstances. He might not look kindly upon a youth whose purse was empty. He might feel Devonny should marry up, rather than down. Therefore Walk must dedicate himself this summer to being sure that Devonny fell in love with him.

Of course, Harriett Ranleigh had the most money of all. Plain women were easy. A few flattering lies and you owned them. But Strat had Harriett by her corset ties. The rich always figured out a way to get richer.

Walk controlled his jealousy, as he had controlled it for so many years, and planned his flirtation with Devonny Stratton.

In the kitchen, the maids washed a cut glass punch bowl so big that two girls had to support it while the third bathed it in soapy water. The raised pineapple designs were cut so sharply they hurt the maids' hands.

The gardener's boys had brought armloads of flowers into the house, and for a moment or two, Florinda supervised the arranging of flowers. But when her friend Genevieve appeared, ready to take a turn around the garden, Florinda called Bridget. "Get my parasol, Bridget. You hold it for me." Florinda's wrists tired easily.

Bridget had not finished polishing. She would get in trouble for not completing the job, but she would get in trouble for not obeying Miss Florinda too. In neither case were excuses permitted. Bridget fetched the parasol, and walked behind the ladies, her arm uncomfortably outstretched to protect Miss Florinda from the sun.

The sun bore down on Bridget's face, however, and multiplied her freckles. Jeb loved her freckles. He had kissed them all, individually. Now there would just be more to kiss.

Bridget permitted herself a huge, cheek-splitting grin of joy when Miss Florinda and Miss Genevieve were not looking. Servants were not permitted emotion.

Harriett and Devonny set up the croquet game, for the grass had dried quickly in the ocean breeze. Strat failed to return, and even Walk wasn't around. The great Mansion felt oddly deserted, and the air felt strangely thin, as though something were about to happen.

"Ladies," said a booming voice.

Harriett steeled herself to be courteous. She knew the voice well. It was Mr. Rowwells, who had some sort of business connection with Strat's father. Naturally the details were never discussed in front of the ladies.

Mr. Rowwells was perhaps ten years older than Harriett, maybe even fifteen. Nobody liked him. Especially Harriett.

Devonny therefore spent lots of time trying to make Mr. Rowwells think Harriett adored him. Harriett had considered throwing Devonny off the tower roof if she did it again, but Devonny just giggled and whispered to Mr. Rowwells that Harriett would probably love to go for a carriage ride with him that evening. It had seemed just a joke between the girls, but now, threatened by Strat's half-dressed young woman, she saw Mr. Rowwells more clearly as a man who wanted a wife.

"Why don't we start our game of croquet," suggested Mr. Rowwells, "since the young gentlemen appear to have started their own game without us."

How fraught with meaning the sentence was. Harriett quivered. Was Mr. Rowwells hinting that Strat's game included a different young lady? Had Mr. Rowwells also seen the bare-legged girl kissing Strat?

Harriett lifted her chin very high. It was a habit that helped keep emotion off her face, providing a slope down which pain and worry would run, like rainwater. "Why, Mr. Rowwells, what a good idea. Devonny, you and Mr. Rowwells be partners. I shall run inside and see who else is available to—"

But they never found a fourth for croquet.

One of the maids began screaming, and from the

windows opened wide for the sea breeze, they heard her curdling shrieks for help.

Mr. Rowwells of course got there first, because Devonny and Harriett were hampered by long skirts and by the corsets that kept them vertical. Mr. Rowwells didn't want the young ladies to see what had happened, and cried that they were to keep their distance. Harriett would have obeyed, but Devonny believed that a thing grown-ups told you to keep a distance from would prove a thing worth seeing, and so she elbowed through the servants, and Harriett followed.

It was one of the servants.

Dead.

He had fallen on the steep dark back stairs that led to the kitchen in the cellar, and he had cracked his skull.

His eyes were open to the ceiling, and spilled on his chest were the sweet cakes and sherry he'd been carrying. The silver tray was half on top of him, like armor.

"Matthew!" cried Devonny, horrified. She tried to go to him, but it was impossible, for he was lying awkwardly upside down on steps too narrow for her to kneel beside him.

Matthew had been with them for years. Every spring when they opened up the Mansion, she was always glad to see Matthew, and see how his children had grown, and give them her old dresses. What a terrible thing! Matthew had five children, only three old enough for grammar school. What would become of them?

Devonny was her father's daughter. Before she was anything else, she was practical. She stared at the glittering silver tray. To whom had Matthew been carrying that?

Certainly not Father. He detested sherry.

Florinda, who adored sherry, was strolling with Genevieve, who had come hoping to get a donation for the Episcopal church. Aunt Ada, had she wanted sherry, would have had to wait for Florinda and Genevieve to return. Would Walker Walkley have dared order sherry? Would Mr. Rowwells?

The stairs were covered with ridged rubber, to prevent slipping. The ceiling was very low, so that the servants had to stoop. The treads of the Great Hall stair formed the ceiling of the kitchen stairs. One tread was rimmed in blood.

"Get up, young lady," snapped Aunt Ada. She took Devonny's arm in pincers like a lobster's, roughly propelling her away from the body. Swiftly Aunt Ada bundled Devonny and Harriett into the library, whose thick doors and solid walls would prevent the girls from learning a single thing.

"The poor babies," whispered Harriett, who had played with them many times, chalking out hopscotch, and twirling jump ropes and sharing cookies. "No father."

No father meant no home. Without Matthew's work here in the Mansion, Devonny's father would not permit that big family to take up space above the stable.

"Do you think Father will provide for the babies, Harry?" Devonny cried, using the old nursery nickname. Harriett was touched, but she knew well, as did Devonny, that Mr. Stratton was not a charitable man.

"It is hardly his responsibility," said Aunt Ada coldly. "These immigrants have far too many children. Your father cannot be expected to concern himself."

Devonny suddenly realized that she hated Aunt Ada. And she was not going to call her "Aunt" anymore. And if Father chose not to be charitable, that didn't mean Devonny had to make the same choice. Well, actually it did, because Devonny could do nothing without her father's permission, but she pretended otherwise. "It is *my* responsibility, then," said Devonny sharply, "and I shall execute it."

Harriett smiled.

Ada's wrinkle-wrapped eyes vanished in a long blink.

The word execute shivered in Devonny's mind like the silver tray. If Matthew had slipped, would he have fallen in that direction? Could the tray have ended up where it did? How did he so totally crush his skull? He had not fallen down the entire flight of stairs. He had evidently been on the top step and simply gone backward. And there was blood on a tread above him—as if his head had been shoved into the upper stair and he had fallen afterward.

Had he been murdered?

Devonny did not repeat this idea to Harriett, who

would only scold her once more about the novels she read. (Harriett read theology and philosophy; Harriett was brilliant; it was a shame she was not a boy, for brains were useless in a lady.)

Devonny certainly could not mention her suspicion to Second Cousin of Somebody Else Ada.

Father?

Father, unfortunately, was the kind of man who believed women had the vapors. Of course, he kept marrying that kind of woman, so he had proof. He would simply tell Devonny to lie down until the sensation passed. He would tell her not to worry her sweet head about such things. He would not be interested in how Matthew died, he would be concerned only that the party and the running of his household not be adversely affected.

She would have to talk to Strat.

Which led Devonny again to the girl on the sand. Devonny knew every houseguest. The girl was not one. So who was she? And where was Strat? And when had Matthew died?

Had the girl on the sand been there?

Had she done it?

Jeb's father did not bother with discussions. Jeb's father was a man of few words, and he had said them once: "Do not step out with the Irish Catholic again." Jeb had not listened. Therefore his father moved from talk to flogging. Jeb hung onto the fence post and set

his teeth tightly to keep the pain inside while his father's leather belt dug into his bare back.

Jeb loved Bridget. She was sweet and hardworking
and her funny Irish accent sang to him, comforting
and bawdy both. He yearned for her.

But she was Catholic. It was a sin against God for
her even to think of becoming Protestant. He would
have to become Catholic. "Why can't we be nothing?"
Jeb had said. Bridget thought less of him after that.

His father stopped. He didn't even wipe the blood
off his belt, just slid it into the pant loops. "Well?"

"I won't see her again," said Jeb.

His father knocked Jeb's jaw upward with a
gnarled fist to see in his son's eyes whether Jeb was
lying. But even Jeb did not know whether he was
lying.

She was tired of him calling her Miss Lockwood.
Strat, however, could not manage anything as familiar
as Annie. So he called her Anna Sophia. "Anna Sophia," he sang, opera style, "Sophia Anna." His deep
bass voice rang out over the road.

Her hair was making him crazy. When they paused
at the corner of Beach and Elm, he could not resist her
hair. He picked it up, making a silken horsetail between his hands, which he twisted on top of her head
the way fashion dictated this year. When he let go, the
hair settled itself. There was not the slightest curl to
the hair; it might have been ironed. He threaded his

fingers through the hair like ribbons. He could not imagine ever touching Harriett's hair like this.

"Where do you live?" he said, because he had to say something, or he would go even farther beyond the rules of behavior.

"Cherry Lane."

He loved her voice. Aunt Ada saw to it that Harriett's voice was carefully modulated. Anna Sophia did not sound like a girl required to modulate anything.

"I don't suppose Cherry Lane is even here," she went on. "It can't be, because our houses were built in the fifties."

Strat was about to argue that plenty of houses had been built in the fifties, until he realized she meant the *nineteen* fifties, which didn't exist.

"The road isn't even paved," she cried. "Not even here in the village."

"Nothing in the country is paved," he said.

"No sidewalks!"

"This is hardly Manhattan."

"What kind of tree is this?"

"It's an elm," he said, "and this is Elm Street."

"Oh, what a shame they all get Dutch elm disease and die," said Miss Lockwood. "They really are beautiful, aren't they?"

Trees? She knew the future of trees? Strat believed neither in time travel nor ghosts, but Anna Sophia was making him think of witches. What power did she have, to know the death of things?

What power did she have to make him shiver every time he looked at her, and never want to do another thing in his life except look at her?

Forget Yale, forget parties, the Mansion, New York.

Strat was out of breath with all the things he no longer cared about.

"There is no Cherry Lane, I was right. But look, Strat. There are cherry trees! It's an orchard. I never knew that. I thought it was just a pretty name, maybe out of Mary Poppins. Our house would be right about there, Strat, where the fence ends."

"Miss Lockwood, you're making me so uncomfortable. I feel as if you really might have come from some other time. Don't talk of death and change."

Don't talk of death and change. Anna Sophia turned back into Annie, whose parents most certainly did not want to talk of death and change. Although in their case, it would be divorce and change. She knew suddenly that Mom knew all about Miss Bartten. Mom knew and had chosen to pretend she didn't, praying praying praying it would go away and they would never have to talk of change or enter a courtroom to accomplish it.

Above them the elms created a beautiful canopy of symmetry and green. Strat eyed them anxiously, after what she had said.

I know the end of the story, she thought. I know the elms will die, but maples will take their place. It's my own story that scares me. I don't know the end of it.

He touched her hair again, drawn like a gold miner to a California stream.

She half recognized where they were. A few buildings were exactly the same as they would be a hundred years later. The ice cream parlor was in a building that no longer existed—the bank parking lot, actually. She did not tell Strat this because he was so proud of the ice cream parlor.

It had no counter, and nobody had cones. It had darling round white tables with tiny delicate chairs. Light and slim as she was, Annie sat carefully, lest the frail white legs of her chair buckle beneath her. Ice cream was served in footed glass compotes sitting on china saucers. Their napkins were cloth, and their spoons silver with souvenir patterns.

Strat could hardly take his eyes off her.

He was forced to do so, however, because his best friend, Walk, as shocked as Strat had been by the girl's clothing and hair and bare legs, came over to be introduced. "Hullo, Walk," said Strat uneasily, getting to his feet. "Miss Lockwood, may I present my school friend, Walker Walkley."

She got up, smiling. "Hey, Walk. Nice to meet you."

Walk practically fell over. He had certainly expected her to call him Mr. Walkley. Strat flushed with embarrassment in spite of ordering himself not to. He half wanted to give Anna Sophia instruction and half wanted her to be just what she was. He fully did not want to be embarrassed in public. Nobody was pretending any longer not to see how unusual this girl was. (Strat preferred the word unusual to words like indecent or unladylike.)

Walk knew perfectly well the last thing Strat wanted was company, so of course he said, "May I join you?"

Why couldn't Walk have stayed at the estate, napping after their baseball game? Why had he come into town for ice cream too? "What a pleasure," said Strat helplessly. Miss Lockwood had already sat down, forgetting the second half of the introductions. "This is Miss Anna Sophia Lockwood, Walk."

"Miss Lockwood," said Walk, bowing slightly before seating himself. "One of the Henry Lockwoods?"

"I think he was a great-grandfather," she agreed.

Strat flinched, but Walk simply assumed he was being given genealogy. Luckily Walk had superior manners. Strat did not want Walk asking how they had met. Walk would never initiate such a topic. Miss Lockwood of course might initiate anything. Strat did not want to share her, and above all, he did not want to share her time travel theory.

He kicked her lightly under the table.

She smiled at him sweetly, a companion in lies. Neatly she settled his own cap back on his head and right there in front of the world—*in the middle of a public ice cream parlor!*—kissed him on the forehead.

It was the kiss of a fallen woman, who would do anything anywhere, and Walker Walkley gasped.

Strat heard nothing. He had never known such a creature existed on this earth, *and she was his.* Strat, too, fell with as much force as if he'd fallen a century.

He fell completely and irrevocably in love with Anna Sophia Lockwood.

*   *   *

The sun set.

Sailboats returned.

The final marshmallows were toasted. Picnic baskets were closed. Tired families trooped over sandy paths to swelteringly hot cars.

The last day of school. And Annie Lockwood had never come home.

Her family tried not to panic. They made the usual phone calls: boyfriend, girlfriend, other girlfriends. The clock moved slowly into the evening, and they began to think of calling the police.

Was it too early to call for help . . . or too late?

CHAPTER 5

"This," said Strat, his voice full, "is my friend, Miss Lockwood."

Harriett, Devonny, Florinda and Genevieve, accustomed to thinking mainly of men, knew immediately what Strat's voice was full of: adoration.

It was worse than Harriett could have dreamed. The girl displayed *bare* legs, *tangled* hair, *no* hat, *tanned* nose and *paint* on her eyelids. There was a gulping silence in which good manners fought with horror. Strat was in love with *this?* This hussy?

Florinda fluttered dangerously. Devonny never allowed Florinda to think she was in charge. The latest stepmother was too feathery in brain, body and clothing to be permitted any leeway. "Florinda, darling," said Devonny, "our poor friend Miss Lockwood has ruined her clothing. I shall just rush her upstairs to borrow some of mine."

Harriett was filled with admiration. Devonny was so quick. And of course fashion was always a good thing, and there was no time when Devonny and Harriett, though six years apart, were not eager to think of clothes. Harriett never visited with fewer than two Saratoga trunks full of costumes, prepared for any possible fashion occasion, and she was even prepared for this one.

"Or my wardrobe," said Harriett. "I think Miss Lockwood is too tall for yours, Dev."

And what a smile Harriett received from Strat. "Oh, would you, Harry? That would be so wonderful! I thank you," he said.

It warmed her that Strat would bring out that little term of endearment. She waited for explanations— who Miss Lockwood was, where she had come from, and why, but Florinda interfered. "Strat, the most dreadful thing has happened. Utterly impossible. I am feeling quite undone."

This was always the case. Harriett was not surprised when Strat didn't bother to ask what dreadful thing. Florinda might not even be thinking of Matthew's death, because she was apt to be overwhelmed if the roses had black spot. Aunt Ada of course had placed herself in charge of the disposal of Matthew's body. This was probably just as well for Strat. He could get Miss Lockwood by Florinda, and Genevieve was a mere beggar passing through, but Aunt Ada would have posed considerable difficulties.

Strat will have to take over the Matthew situation, Harriett said to herself, and perhaps he will forget about Miss Lockwood. I can shut her in a tower and throw away the key.

This sounded wonderful. Harriett didn't even feel guilty. At least Miss Lockwood would have a smashing gown to wear during her imprisonment.

It was of no interest to Walker Walkley that a servant had fallen on the stairs. Walk's mind was seething with new plans. What great good fortune that after baseball he'd cycled straight down to the village. Strat had actually taken the little hussy home with him. Astounding how stupid men would become when their minds were overtaken by physical desire.

Walk understood the fun that lay ahead for Strat. Walk had worked through his own household maids, having gotten two with child. Those babies were disposed of through the orphanages and the girls themselves sent on to other households. Walk's father was proud of him.

There was to be a huge party tonight. Strat never even glanced at Harriett, not even when he thanked her for offering her own wardrobe. Walk studied Harriett. The lovesick expression in Strat's eyes was very hurtful to her.

Perhaps, thought Walker Walkley, a little consolation is in order for Harriett. Me.

Forget Devonny. Anyway, Devonny had a rebellious streak, the kind that must be thoroughly crushed in females. Mr. Stratton senior, who had spent his life crushing everyone in sight, indulged Devonny. De-

71

vonny would prove a difficult wife. Harriett, plain and desperate, was obedient . . . and much, much richer.

He exulted, thinking of her money, her land, her houses, her corporations, her stocks and bonds and gold and silver. Mine, thought Walker Walkley. Mine!

Harriett would bear the children Walk required, and be an effective mother. Meanwhile, he would also have all the fun he required. That's what women were for.

The key was to help Strat with his little hoyden. Walk must make it easy for Strat. Then Walk would dance with Harriett. Walk understood homely ladies. Offer them a ring and a rose and mention marriage and they were yours.

Keep it up, Miss Lockwood! thought Walker Walkley, retiring to his room to prepare for the evening. He closed the door behind himself, and leaned against it, laughing with glee.

Annie, too, believed that fashion was always a good thing. She had been awestruck by what the other girls at that ice cream parlor had had on, and could hardly wait to have clothes like that herself.

Somehow Strat had gotten her into the Mansion without explanations. In 1995, these two girls, Harriett and Devonny, would have peppered her with questions; it would have been like *Oprah* or *Donahue*. *Yeah, so waddaya think you're doin' here, Annie?*

But in 1895, they simply stared with falling-open mouths at the sight of Annie's bra. It was her prettiest.

Pale lavender with hot pink splashes of color, like a museum painting of flowers.

Devonny gasped. "Where—what—I mean—I haven't—"

Harriett said quickly, "We can lace her into something decent."

And they did.

Annie would never have submitted to it, except that Harriett and Devonny showed her they were wearing the same thing. It was, thought Annie, a wire cage you could keep canaries in. The cage was flexible, and by hauling on cords fastened to each rib of the cage, they tightened it on her. It completely changed the shape of her body. Her waist grew smaller and smaller, and where it had all been crammed, Annie was not sure until she could no longer breathe. "You squished my lungs together," she protested. "What's happening to my kidneys and my heart? I can't breathe!"

"Of course you can," said Harriett. "Just carefully."

"Why are we doing this?"

"Fashion," said Harriett.

"Don't you faint all the time from lack of oxygen?"

"Of course," said Devonny. "It's very feminine."

"Does Strat approve?"

"Strat?" repeated Devonny. "My goodness. How long have you known my brother?"

Annie had forgotten they called each other Miss and Mister. I'm missing my cue lines, she thought. I must work harder to fit into the century. How long *have* I known Strat? I didn't bring a watch into this century. "Two or three hours, I think," she said.

Considering the circumstances, the girls chattered quite easily. Devonny and Harriett had apparently decided she was from some low part of town. A branch of the Lockwood family that had intermarried and grown extra fingers and forgotten how to wear corsets, probably licked their dinner plates instead of washing them. It was clear that anything Hiram Stratton, Jr., wanted, he got. Even a half-naked townie.

The door opened.

There was no knock first. In came a girl in a brown-checked ankle-length dress covered by an enormous white apron. The apron was starched so much it could have stood alone. It was hard to guess the girl's age. Her hands were raw like old women who scrubbed all day and never used lotion. Her face, though, was very pretty, remarkably fair complexioned. She had black hair, black eyes and a sparkly, excited look to her.

Devonny and Harriett did not say hello, nor even look over. She might have been a houseplant.

"Miss Devonny," scolded the girl in a melodious voice, half singing, "how could you start dressing without me?" Not a houseplant. A housemaid.

Annie was awestruck. Devonny's own maid there to dress her! Clicking her tongue, the maid relaced Annie tight enough to crack ribs. Then she quickly and expertly lowered a pale yellow underdress over Annie's head. She had never worn anything so soft and satiny against her skin.

Devonny and Harriet sorted through Harriett's gowns.

"Here." Harriett produced a daffodil-yellow dress festooned like a Christmas tree, sleeves billowing out like helium balloons around her shoulders, and looping white lace like popcorn strings. Annie felt like an illustration of Cinderella.

Ooooh, this is so neat! she thought. And I get to dance at the ball too! I wonder what happens at midnight.

"Bridget, what shall we do with her hair?" said Devonny.

The maid brushed Annie's hair hard, holding it in her hands as Strat had done. Annie adored having somebody play with her hair. Bridget looped it, pinned it, fluffed it, until it piled like a dark, cloudy ruffle. Bridget released tiny wisps, which she wet and curled against Annie's cheeks.

She stared at herself in the looking glass. A romantic, old-fashioned beauty stared back.

Annie Lockwood decided right then and there to stay in this century. A belle of the ball, where men bow and ladies wear gloves. Of course, without oxygen, she was not sure how long she'd survive. If only somebody could take a photograph for her to carry home and show off.

Annie stole a look at Harriett's dressing table. Creams to soften the skin and perfumes from France, weaponlike hat pins and hair combs encrusted with jewels, but no eye shadow, no mascara and no lipstick. She had so much clothing on, layer after layer, and yet her face felt naked. Nobody suggested makeup. They don't wear makeup, thought Annie. What else don't they do?

It occurred to her, creepily, that perhaps the photo of her had already been taken and she herself, a hundred years from now, would find it in some historical society file.

Music had begun: the very harp she had heard falling through. From downstairs came the clamor and laughter of guests. Annie could smell cigars and pipes, hear the clatter of horses' hooves and wooden wheels and the laughter of flirting women.

Every wish had arrived, exactly the way Annie had daydreamed. She would dance with Strat, so unlikely and so handsome and gallant. She would pin a yellow rose on this dress fit for an inaugural ball, flirt with men in frock coats, drink from crystal goblets and laugh behind a feathered fan.

"I will be introducing you, I expect," said Harriett. "I fear I'm not quite sure what to say, Miss Lockwood."

"Anna Sophia Lockwood," Annie told her. The name she had despised all her life sounded elegant and formal, like the dress.

"Yes, but people will want to know—well—"

"I'm just here briefly," said Annie. She wanted these girls to share the mystery and astonishment. "Tell your guests that I'm passing through on a longer journey. A journey through time."

Harriett stared.

Devonny interlocked her fingers within long white gloves.

Bridget shivered and stepped back. "Are you," whispered Bridget, "some sort of witch?"

How ancient was Bridget's accent. How foreign. Annie lost track of the century. Had she fallen deeper than she'd thought? Was she caught in a place where witches were burned or hung? Where was Strat?

Maybe I am a witch, thought Annie, because what power could let me, and no other, travel through time?

Fear trapped the girls.

She had been a fool to hint at the time travel.

The best defense is a good offense, she reminded herself. If it's good enough for a field hockey locker room, it's good enough for a Victorian dressing room. "I'm just a Lockwood," she said lightly. "And you, Bridget?"

"I'm a Shanrahan, miss," said Bridget.

"She's Irish," said Harriett, as if saying, She's sub-human.

Bridget flushed and began to dress Miss Harriett. The petticoat of silk draped over Harriett's cage was a treasure, vivid pink, ribboned and ruffled. Next Bridget lowered a gown of hotter pink over it. Harriett's gown was fit for a princess. It was awesome.

And Harriett, poor Harriett, was not. She just wasn't pretty.

Annie's heart broke for all plain girls in all centuries. In the looking glass, as huge and beveled as every other mirror in this great house, she saw the terrible contrast between herself and Harriett. "You're very kind to help me like this," Annie told her.

Harriett seemed out of breath. The corset, Annie

thought. We women are crazy. Imagine agreeing to strap yourself into a canary cage before you appear in public.

"I saw you, Miss Lockwood!" cried Harriett. "From the tower. You and Strat."

A century might have fallen away, but Annie knew everything now: Harriett was in love with Strat and terrified of losing him. Annie wanted to console Harriett, who was being so kind to her, saying, Oh, it was nothing, just plain old garden-variety friendship.

But they had not been plain.

I almost possess Strat, thought Annie. Harriett knows that. His sister, Devonny, knows that. Perhaps the maid Bridget knows too. He is almost mine. If I stay . . . Strat . . . the Mansion . . . the roses and the gowns and the servants . . . they would be mine too.

She had a curious triangular thought, like the mirrors, that she must look at this only from her own point of view. If she let herself think of Harriett . . . But this is only a game, she thought, a dream or an electrical storm. No need to think of anybody else.

Bridget dabbed perfume on Annie's throat and wrists and produced the gloves with which her hands would stay covered all evening. The scent of lilacs filled Annie's thoughts and she was seized by terror.

What if she *was* on a longer journey?

What if—when she was ready to leave—*she left in the wrong direction?* What if she fell backward another hundred years? Or another thousand? *What if she could not get home?*

She looked out a window to remind herself of the constancy of sky and sun, but the window was stained glass: a cathedral of roses and ivy; you could not look through it, only at it.

A clock chimed nine times and Annie thought: *I'm not home.*

Mom is home now, and Tod and Daddy, supper is over, and I'm not there. They've called Heather, and they've called Kelly, and I'm not there. They've called Sean and he'll say, Well, she was at the beach for a while but I don't know what happened to her next. They'll get scared around the edges. At the edges will be the horrible things: drowning, kidnapping, runaways, murder, rape. Nobody will say those words out loud.

But it's getting dark. And it will get darker, and so will my mother's fears.

Harriett put both arms around Annie. "Are you all right, Miss Lockwood? You looked terrified. Please don't be afraid. You're among friends."

"Oh, Harriett," said Annie Lockwood, "you're such a nice person." She was overcome with guilt. I can't do this to Harriett, she thought. But I want Strat, too. And I must have fallen through time for a reason. It must be Strat.

Walker Walkley caught the little Irish maid in the hallway and swung her into his room. "Mr. Walkley," she protested, "I have work to do."

"Spend a little time with me first," said Walk, putting his hands where Bridget did not even let Jeb put hands.

Bridget removed his hands and glared at him.

How pretty she was, fired up like that. Walk grinned. He put his hands right back where he wanted them to be.

"Please, Mr. Walkley." The maid struggled to be courteous. She could not lose her position.

Walk laughed and continued. She'd enjoy it once they got started.

Bridget had few weapons, but she used one of them. She spit on him. Her saliva ran down his face.

Oh! it made Bridget so angry! America was perfect, but Americans weren't. These men who thought she was property!

"Touch me, Mr. Walkley," said Bridget Shanrahan, "and I will shove you down the stairs and you'll die like Matthew."

Walker Walkley wiped his cheek with his white handkerchief, nauseated and furious. She had made an enemy.

And said a very dumb thing.

"And are we prepared?" said Aunt Ada.

"We are prepared."

"The little Lockwood creature is the answer to my prayers," said Aunt Ada. "I needed a solution, and moments later, it occurred."

Ada prayed often, and read her Bible thoroughly. It was a rare occasion on which she felt that even God cared whether she had what she needed. Now, so late in life that she had reached the rim of despair, had a guardian angel finally appeared for her too?

It was a nice thought. Ada studied her hands as if they were wands that accomplished things against nature. "Lust has power," she said. "We'll encourage the boy to enjoy himself. We need only an evening or two."

Their smiles slanted with the need for money.

Miss Lockwood had been beautiful on the beach, the wind curving her hair against his face, but here in the ballroom Strat thought she was the loveliest female he had ever seen. The men were envious of him, and lined up for the chance to partner with her.

She had not known any of the dances, but she'd proved a quick learner, willing to laugh at herself. Right there in the ballroom, without a blush, she let each partner teach her another step. She was so light on her feet. She and Strat had spun around the room like autumn leaves falling from trees: at one with the wind and the melody. Now she was dancing with Walk, and Strat was so jealous he could hardly breathe.

"Strat, I have to talk to you," said Devonny in his ear.

Strat didn't want to talk. He wanted to dance with Miss Lockwood now and forever. He didn't want his little sister placing demands and awaiting explanations. He could not explain Miss Lockwood, he just couldn't. It would sound as if he had had too much to drink or started on opium. Time travel, indeed; 1995, indeed.

"Look at me, Strat, so I'll know you're on this planet. We have three subjects we have to cover."

Sisters were such a pain.

"First, you have to be nice to Harriett. Don't you see you're destroying her?"

He had not thought once of Harriett since he had met Miss Lockwood. He did not want to think of her now. If he looked Harriett's way, he'd get back some reproachful expression. I haven't made any promises. I haven't even made any suggestions. I have nothing to feel guilty about, Strat told himself.

Guilt swarmed up and heated his face.

"Second, who is she, this Miss Lockwood?" Devonny tapped a silk-shod foot on the floor for emphasis.

"She's a friend, Dev," he said, "and that's all I'm going to say for now."

His sister looked at him long and hard.

"What's three?" he said quickly.

"Matthew was murdered."

CHAPTER 6

"Devonny, you mustn't bother your little head about it," said her brother. "It's bad for you." He smiled that infuriating male smile, telling her she was a girl and had to obey. Nothing got Devonny madder faster. This was when she knew she was going to wear trousers after all, and be fast, and bad, and scandalous. Show Father and Strat a thing or two.

Which made her madder? Saying her head was little, or that Matthew's death didn't matter enough to bother?

Men! They—

But it was a new world, with new tools, and it occurred to Devonny she could go around her father and brother.

Other hearts in that ballroom beat with love and hope, jealousy and pain. Devonny's beat with terror and excitement. What would Father do to her? It would be worth it just to see!

Devonny slipped out of the ballroom and crossed the Great Hall to the cloakroom. Here she approached the machine nervously. She did not often have the opportunity to touch the telephone. Young ladies wrote notes. Servants responded when the telephone rang, and servants took and delivered messages.

Devonny gathered her courage.

Harriett was left stranded. She had no partner. It was unthinkable. Strat was blind tonight, and Harriett was both furious and deeply humiliated. How they all looked at her, the other ladies; each of them prettier; and how they looked at Miss Lockwood, the prettiest of all.

She saw Walker Walkley feeling sorry for her. Any moment now Walk would rescue her, and she hated it, that she was plain and needed rescue. How could Strat put her in this position! Why did there have to be Miss Lockwoods? Harriett hoped Miss Lockwood rolled down the hill and drowned in the ocean.

Walk moved toward her from his side of the ballroom, and Mr. Rowwells approached from the opposite side. I don't want to be pitied, thought Harriett, I want to be loved. I don't want anybody to be kind to me. I'd rather be a spinster. An old maid.

But then she would be like Aunt Ada. Mean to people because life had been mean to her.

Oh, Strat, thought Harriett, fighting off tears she

could not bear to have anybody see. Please remember me. Please love me.

"My dear Miss Harriett," said Mr. Rowwells, "might I have the pleasure of a stroll with you? Perhaps a turn on the veranda? The evening air is delightful."

Well, she would rather be rescued by Mr. Rowwells, who meant and who knew nothing, than by Walk, who knew everything. Harriett bowed slightly and rested her glove on his arm. Her guardian, Mr. Stratton senior, said that Mr. Rowwells was a fine schemer, an excellent capitalist. Mr. Rowwells had made a fortune in lumber, but one doubted he could make a fortune in his new venture. He actually thought mayonnaise could be put in jars and sold.

Mr. Rowwells was trying to get investors, but men with money burst out laughing. Women needed things to do, so even if you could put mayonnaise in a jar, you'd just be taking away their chores. A woman with time on her hands was a dangerous thing. (Except of course women like Florinda, who could not be given chores in the first place, because of delicacy.)

Mr. Rowwells chatted about small things and Harriett tried to be interested, but wasn't.

In June the garden air was so heavy with rose perfume that ladies were claiming to be faint from it. Harriett felt faint too, but not from perfume.

Perhaps it is a good thing that I love books and knowledge, thought Harriett. I will go to college, since I cannot have Strat.

She had never met a female who had attended such an institution. The mere thought of going away from home was so frightening that she felt faint all over again.

I would be twenty-four when I emerge, and might as well be dead. Nobody will marry me if I'm that old.

Harriett had been taught to hide her intelligence. She could of course imitate the first Mrs. Stratton, reading at home, becoming an expert on Homer and the Bible, able to recite Shakespeare and Milton and Wordsworth. But in exchange for being better educated than Mr. Stratton, Strat and Devonny's mother found herself divorced and replaced.

A very very bad part of Harriett had a solution to the problem of Miss Lockwood. She would introduce Miss Lockwood to Mr. Stratton senior. Even for him it would be quite an age difference—he was *fifty* now! But rapidly tiring of Florinda. Yes. Harriett would seize that flirty little Miss Anna Sophia and wrap her little hand inside Mr. Stratton's great cruel fingers and—

No. It was too nauseating. Harriett didn't wish on anybody the prison of being wife number five for Mr. Stratton.

I just want to be wife number one for Strat, she thought.

Mr. Rowwells soldiered on, trying to find topics. Since Harriett was considering only the possible death or dismemberment of Miss Lockwood, Mr. Rowwells wasn't getting anywhere.

"What does interest you, my dear? Surely you and I have something in common!" Mr. Rowwells patted her hand. In situations like this, Harriett was always glad to have gloves on.

"I am interested in scholarship, Mr. Rowwells. I wish to continue my education. I have thought of requesting Mr. Stratton to permit me to attend a women's college."

"College?" repeated Mr. Rowwells. She had stunned him, and she liked that.

"I would be well chaperoned," explained Harriett, lest Mr. Rowwells think she was a guttersnipe like Miss Lockwood.

"Capital idea!" he said. "I will encourage your guardian. And of course, Miss Ada would accompany you. You have a great mind, Miss Harriett."

What was wrong with God, to let a girl be born with brains instead of beauty?

"I'm sure you are well acquainted with the classics," said Mr. Rowwells. "Perhaps you could instruct me."

"Why, Mr. Rowwells, I would love to share my favorite books with you," she said, and she almost meant it; she almost wanted to sit with him and discuss books, which were safe, instead of love, which was not. Harriett blushed, imagining what Strat and Miss Lockwood would talk of.

"The color in your cheeks becomes you," Mr. Rowwells complimented. "The color of the roses by the fountain."

Oh, how she wanted to look becoming.

They walked to the far edge of the garden where no gaslights illuminated the darkness. "The moon is rising over the ocean, Harriett. It's shining in your hair."

"It is?" said Harriett eagerly.

*　　*　　*

On the back stairs, Bridget was forced to step over and over on the bloodstains where Matthew had died. She could hardly put her foot there. Miss Ada had slapped her for showing tears in front of the guests. She had a handprint on her cheek now.

I must think of nothing but service, Bridget told herself, nothing but doing my work, finishing the tasks, not looking where I put my shoe.

But the cook had news.

"What?" gasped Bridget. "Already? Matthew's not cold yet, and Mr. Stratton's told the family to leave?"

"It's true," said the cook, who'd been crying, like all the staff.

Mr. Stratton had to know that Matthew's wife had nowhere to go. And no money to pay for it.

"What a wicked man," said Bridget. "They're all wicked. Mr. Walkley is wicked."

"He try to yank you into his room?" said the cook knowingly.

"I spit on him," said Bridget.

"You should have laughed and slipped off with a smile. He'll get you for it."

Bridget had been sick with fear imagining herself out on the street. But if she had five babies, what would she do? She must think about them, not herself. "Young Mr. Stratton isn't cruel," said Bridget. "I'll tell him about Matthew's family. He won't let them be put out."

"Glued to that girl, he is. Can't hear a word being

said. Poor Miss Harriett. She's about to die herself. The only one in this family who could help is Miss Devonny. She has spunk."

Bridget went upstairs to refill the punch bowl. Beautifully gowned women and handsomely dressed men flirted and schemed and danced. Nobody saw Bridget because servants were invisible. The problem of Matthew had been made invisible, and soon the problem of Matthew's family would be made invisible.

Jeb, marry me, prayed Bridget. Mother of God, tell Jeb to marry me and take me away from these awful people.

The man with the greatest temper also had the greatest bulk. Mr. Stratton senior had spent much of his fifty years consuming fine food and wine. He was so angry he could hardly see his son. "Stop prancing around with that girl, Strat. You know quite well, young man, what is expected of you."

"Father, please. She's a wonderful person, she—"

"The personality, or lack of it, in your little tramp doesn't matter. You march back in there and spend the evening with Harriett."

Strat could not ignore Miss Lockwood. He had told her he would take care of her and he had meant it. He had never meant anything more. It terrified Strat to talk back to his father. How did Devonny do it so easily? "She isn't a tramp, Father."

Hiram Stratton's flat eyes drilled into his son's.

"Oh? Who are her parents? Where did she come from? Why is she unchaperoned?"

Strat never considered mentioning another century to his father. He'd been beaten several times in childhood and had no desire to repeat the experience. Young men headed to Yale and expecting to control enormous fortunes could not run around babbling that they were in love with creatures from the next century. Forget whipping; he might find himself in an asylum chained to a wall.

"Father, she was down on the beach. I realize I shouldn't have befriended a stranger. But I was drawn to her. She's a wonderful, interesting, beautiful—"

His father gestured irritably. "Maids like Bridget exist for a man's entertainment, Strat. No doubt that's what your Miss Lockwood is, somebody's maid sneaking around our beach on her day off. But a man enjoys himself quietly. He certainly does not offend a wealthy young woman who hopes to marry him."

Strat could not think.

Thinking, actually, did not interest him in the slightest right now. His thoughts were so physical he was shocked by them. He could never have expressed them to his father. He did not know how he was going to express them to Miss Lockwood. And there was no way he could make a detour and put Harriett Ranleigh first.

The lines in his father's face grew deeper and harsher, as if his father were turning into a monster before his eyes. "Here are your instructions," said his father in a very soft, very controlled voice. He leaned down, beard first, thrusting gray and black wire into Strat's face. "Wipe that dream off your face and out of your heart. You go out there now, and ask Harriett to dance, and spend the remainder of this evening dancing with her and be sure that the two of you have made plans for tomorrow before you say good night. And your good night to Harriett Ranleigh is to be affectionate and meaningful. Do you understand me?"

If he did not hold on to Miss Lockwood, she would fall back through. Like Cinderella, she would vanish at midnight, but she would leave no glass slipper, and he could never find her again. "Father," he began.

His father spoke so softly it was like hearing from God. "You will obey me."

I can't! I love her too much. I would give up anything for her.

"Answer me," said his father.

"Sir," said Hiram Stratton, Jr., bowing slightly to his father, and escaping from the library, without adding either a yes or a no.

The walls of the ballroom were lined not only with splintered mirrors, but with old women. Terrifying old. Annie did not think people got that old in 1995; or perhaps they got that old, but continued to look young. These women looked like a coven of witches: women with sagging cheeks, ditch-deep wrinkles, thin graying hair and angry eyes.

They were the chaperons.

Each was an escort to a beautiful young girl, and jealousy radiated from their unlovely bodies.

The one who chaperoned Harriett had locked eyes with Annie. Behind her missing teeth and folded lips, the old woman was gleeful with knowledge Annie did not possess.

The sexes were separated and stylized like drawings come to life. Yet in spite of how formal these people were, in spite of their manners and mannerisms, the room reeked emotion, swirling beneath feet and through hearts.

Strat led her through another dance, and she followed, and the room felt as thick as her brain. Thick velvet, thick damask, thick scent of flowers, thick fringe dripping from every drape.

Strat himself seemed desperate, engulfed in some drama of his own, hiding it with manners. Slowly, he danced her out the glass doors and onto the veranda. Far off, where the village must be, not a single light twinkled.

No electricity, thought Annie, waking from the trance of the ballroom.

Strat had enough electricity for two. His eyes stroked her as his hands could not. "Let's walk down the holly lane," he said. "We have to talk about—"

"Capital idea," said Walk, suddenly appearing next to them, his smile as sly and gleeful as the chaperon's. "Midnight! And a stroll. James! Miss Van Vleet! Miss Stratton! Richard! Strat here wants a midnight ramble under the stars."

"How delightful!" cried Miss Van Vleet.

"Might I take your arm?" offered James to Miss Van Vleet.

"Where is Harriett?" said Walk. His eyes were hot and full of meaning when he looked at Strat. "We mustn't go without Harriett."

Strat flinched.

"Miss Ranleigh is in the library with Mr. Rowwells," said Aunt Ada. Her face was wrinkled like linen waiting for the iron. "Do go without her. She won't mind at all."

The young people paired up. Nobody walked alone. It was unthinkable that a girl should be without a boy's arm. How sweet they looked in the soft yellowy gaslight, like a sepia photograph on a relative's wall.

Walker Walkley took Devonny's arm after all. His smile, like the crone's, seemed to have more knowledge than a smile should.

He's sly, thought Annie. I don't trust him.

The weird enclosure of the stays kept her posture extremely vertical. Since she couldn't bend at the waist, it was necessary to hang onto Strat when the party descended the steep hill.

Perhaps I'm in both places at one time, thought Annie. Perhaps my 1995 self is turning off the television and getting ready for bed.

The topic was whether young ladies should be educated.

"I am going to college," said Devonny.

"Nonsense," said Walk. "Too much knowledge is

not good for the health. A woman's place is in the home, obedient to her husband or father. You wouldn't let Devonny go, would you, Strat?"

Strat seemed to reach the topic from afar. Eventually he said, "I believe they're quite strict at a female college. Chapel every day, of course. Chaperons. Harriett has also talked about it. She yearns to learn more."

"Harriett has learned too much already," said James grumpily.

Miss Van Vleet mentioned the newly formed Red Cross. She expressed a shy interest in helping the downtrodden.

"Oh, Gertrude!" cried Devonny, forgetting education. "That's so wonderful, I would love to do that! I am so impressed. I would—"

"No," said Strat sharply. "Neither Father nor I would permit such a thing."

How astonishing that Strat thought it was his business. Even more astonishing that pretty Miss Van Vleet was actually Gertrude. These people did not know how to pick names.

The gentlemen discussed how much control brothers should exert over their sisters.

Should her brother, Tod, ever dream of taking charge of Annie, he would end up in the emergency room, she decided. And then, less proudly, realized that Sean controlled her as fully as the Stratton men controlled Devonny. And I let him, she thought.

The others romped on ahead.

94

She was blessedly alone with Strat.

How dark it was. The moon was a delicate crescent, the way everything here seemed so delicate, so polite.

Strat was like a perfect toy. A birthday gift. How delightful that Time had given him to her!

She flung her arms around this wonderful boy, and Strat became real: the whole thing became real; he was not a toy, but a frantic young man who simply adored her.

Strat stopped himself from kissing her and stepped back. "We cannot," he said, all self-control. "People would say things, Miss Lockwood. I cannot allow them to say things about you."

The way he said that pronoun, you, took Annie Lockwood over the edge. When she had fallen through time, she had felt a roaring in her ears, but now the roaring was within. Heart and mind collapsed. The falling, this time, was into love.

If she had had a fainting couch, she would have used it, and pulled Strat down on top of her. "Who cares about people's opinions?" She began laughing with the joy of it. "I love you, Strat."

He touched her cheeks with shy fingers. Then he took her hand, the glove between them delicate cottony lace that was barely there, and yet completely there.

I, too, thought Annie, am barely here. Don't let midnight come! Don't let this be a magic spell that ends. *I love him.* Love is for always. Please.

Strat, who wore no canary cage, was having as much trouble finding enough oxygen as Annie. They gasped alternately, like conversation.

"I care about their opinions," said Strat finally. "And I care about you. There are rules. You must obey the rules."

Strat's rules made him keep walking to join the rest of the party; it would damage Annie's reputation, perhaps, to be alone with him in the night even for a minute.

"Do you have a choice?" said Strat suddenly. "Coming and going? If you have to return, and return quickly, can you choose to? How did it come, the time traveling? Please tell me about yourself." His voice ached like a lover's. He needed details.

"Oh, Strat, I have a wonderful family but they're not doing very well right now. My father loves somebody else and I don't know what to do."

Strat nodded. "My father nearly always loves somebody else, and his wives never know what to do either. Then he tells them they're being divorced and that settles that."

"Will you be that kind of husband?"

He shook his head. He mumbled things, words of love and marriage, rules and promises.

He wants to marry me, thought Annie Lockwood, dumbfounded. I am actually standing with a man who is thinking of marriage. To me.

For Strat, a promise was made of steel, and a rule of iron. How beautiful. He had virtue. He followed the rules in order to be right. To be righteous. Men and rules. If Daddy had obeyed the rules, if he had restricted himself the way these people do, my family would be all right.

The clippy-cloppy of horses' hooves and the metallic clunking of high thin-spoked wheels interrupted the night.

"It's the police cab!" shouted Walk joyfully, running back toward the Mansion. He whopped Strat on the back as he loped past. Some things didn't change over the century. Boys showed their friendship by hitting each other. Annie was never going to understand that one. "They think Matthew was pushed, you know. Utter tripe, of course, that sort of thing would never happen here, but some immigrant with a hot temper might have done it. They're letting anybody into the country now."

Strat said they couldn't go back if the police were there, they had the ladies to think of.

If he knew the cop shows I watch on TV, thought Annie, what would he think? I who probably know a thousand times more about violence than he does.

"The ladies, thank you," said Devonny, "are just as interested, and this lady happens to be the one who telephoned the police. So there."

"You used the telephone?" said her brother, equally impressed and furious. "You spoke to the police? Did you have Father's permission?"

"Of course not. He wasn't interested. He said it was an unfortunate accident and even if it *wasn't* an unfortunate accident it was *going* to be an unfortunate accident."

Annie grinned, liking Devonny, thinking what friends they could be.

"What are we talking about?" demanded Miss Van Vleet. "Who is Matthew? Why was it not an unfortunate accident?"

"Matthew," said Devonny, "is a servant. His little girls get my old dresses. Matthew died on the stairs. I felt, from the force and violence of the wounds to his skull, and the fact that there was blood above the body, that it was not caused by gravity. Matthew was murdered."

"Oooooh!" said Miss Van Vleet, thrilled. "I'm sure you've been reading too many novels, Devonny. But let's hurry."

They hurried, while Strat and Annie hurried a little less, and were momentarily in their own dark world again.

"I love you, Miss Lockwood."

"Annie," she corrected him.

"Annie," he repeated softly, the intimacy of that name a privilege to him. "I'll take care of you, Annie. I won't let anybody hurt you. I won't let anything happen. I promise."

He kissed her cheek. It was not the kiss of a brother or friend. It was definitely not the kiss of movies or backseats. It was not conversation, and yet it stated such intent, such purpose.

If anything had ever been "sealed with a kiss," it

was this moment between this boy and this girl on that lane by the sea.

I won't be going back, thought Annie.

I'm here.

And I'm his.

CHAPTER 7

He had disobeyed. Sons had been disinherited for less. How was he going to make up to Harriett for this, and still have Miss Lockwood, and not get in trouble with his father?

Anna Sophia danced her way up the Great Hill. Strat had told her not to worry, everything would be all right, and she had believed him. If I can get her by Father and Ada, thought Strat, then in the morning . . . In the morning, what?

No solutions came to mind.

When the young people reached the porte cochere, the police cabriolet still there, tired horses quiet and motionless, the police themselves were not in evidence. Mr. Hiram Stratton, Sr., was not about to allow his houseguests to be concerned with a nasty and trivial affair. The police had been sent to the basement and kitchens, which, after all, were Matthew's domain. And

Hiram Stratton, Sr., thank the dear Lord, was also in the basement, telling the police what to do and when to do it.

Strat's stepmother fluttered and dipped in front of him like a chicken losing feathers. Her corsage drooped and her hair was falling out of its pins.

"Hullo, Florinda," said Strat. "Which room have you given to Miss Lockwood?"

Florinda swooped and worried. "Which room?" she repeated nervously.

"The French Room, of course," said Devonny, glaring at her brother. "Come, Miss Lockwood. I'll show you the way. Florinda, you needn't think about it again."

Florinda was relieved. So were Devonny and Strat, because Father wouldn't know. "Until morning, anyway," Devonny muttered to her brother.

"Did Father tell you what my orders were?" whispered Strat.

"Of course not. But I live here, Strat. I know what your orders were, and I agree with them. You should have escorted Harriett. But I don't want Miss Lockwood sleeping on the sand, so I'll put her in the French Room, and in any event, I expect when I confess that mine was the unidentified female voice telephoning the police, Father will be too angry with me to remember you. It'll pass by as long as you send Miss Lockwood home in the morning."

Things always look better in the morning. Father can't do anything to or about Anna Sophia now. I don't have to worry till morning.

He wanted a good night kiss, the kind lovers give each other behind closed doors, but he was in the Great Hall, and Walker Walkley was watching, and Florinda was fluttering, and James was curious, so Strat merely smiled in a detached way and Devonny whisked Miss Lockwood up the great stairs.

Miss Lockwood's fingers grazed the bulging eyes of the walnut gargoyles, and Strat shivered, for his father could just as easily graze her life, and change it. For the worse.

The second floor was dark and wondrous. Chandeliers of yellow gaslight illuminated walls papered in gold. Niches were filled with feather bouquets and stuffed birds and marble statuettes. The pretty little maid reappeared. Her apron was stained now, the starch out of it. Bridget looked exhausted.

"Miss Lockwood," said Devonny crisply, "will need the loan of my nightclothes. She will use the French Room. You may retire when Miss Lockwood and I are abed. And you are not again to wear a soiled uniform in my presence, Bridget."

"Yes, miss. I'm sorry, miss." Her voice sounded as whipped as her body looked. Bridget escorted Annie into a huge and utterly fabulous bedroom, fit for a princess. Bridget shut the door neatly behind them and matter of factly began to undress Annie.

The clothing Harriet had loaned her was not one-person clothing. You could not undo fifty tiny buttons down your back. You could not untie your own laces.

You could not lift your gown over your head by yourself. It was like a wedding gown; you needed bridesmaids to deal with the very dress.

Bridget now lowered a nightgown over Annie, soft ivory with tucks and ruches and pleats. It was fit for a trousseau, but then, so was everything Annie had seen.

The private bathroom was surprisingly similar to her own at home, but immensely larger, with fixtures of gold. The tub could have held an entire family. The marble sink did have hot water, and the toilet, bless its heart, flushed.

Bridget brushed Annie's hair over and over: a massage of the scalp and the soul. Everybody should be pampered like this, thought Annie. Of course, nobody will do it for Bridget, and that's where it all breaks down, but I might as well enjoy it anyway.

Every stroke of the brush moved her closer and closer to sleep. Bridget tucked her in as if she were two instead of sixteen. The bed was so thickly soft she expected to suffocate when she reached bottom. What if I fall back home again while I'm asleep? she thought dimly. What if I don't wake up at the Mansion, but a century later?

What if—

But sleep claimed her, and she knew nothing of the night at all.

She did not hear the police leave.

She did not hear Bridget staggering up to the attic after an eighteen-hour day.

And nobody heard Harriett weep, for she smothered her tears in her pillow.

*   *   *

Devonny had a morning gown sent to her room. Annie loved that. You had your evening gowns, so of course you had to have your morning gowns. Why hadn't she ever had a morning gown before?

Her morning gown was simply cut, waist higher and sleeves less puffy. She coaxed Bridget not to lace her up so tightly. Breathing was good and Victorian women did not do enough of it. Florinda did practically none at all, which was doubtless why she kept fainting.

Breakfast was quite wonderful.

This, thought Annie, is the way to live. Everyone should have a screened veranda high on a hill, with views of the ocean and a lovely soft breeze. Everyone should have servants too. You snap your fingers and they bring anything you want. I approve of this world.

It seemed odd to have no radio: no morning talk show, no traffic report, no news of the world.

There was a newspaper, but only for the men. The gentlemen had chosen to have breakfast indoors, in the formal dining room. Annie caught a glimpse of them, but they had not bothered to catch a glimpse of her. Women had their moments of importance, but not now.

How little Strat resembled his father—thank goodness. His father was corpulent, big rolls of him sagging beneath his great black jacket and white pleated shirt, with a mustache that crawled into his mouth and eyebrows that crawled on his forehead. Annie tried to imagine the pretty little cloud wisp that was Florinda actually choosing to marry this gross man. How very badly Florinda must have needed the shelter and money that Hiram Stratton provided.

Miss Van Vleet, Mr. Innings, Mr. Walkley, Florinda and Genevieve were not up yet. The four of them, Harriett, Devonny, Strat and Annie, were dining together as if they always did.

Harriett was having coffee and a single waffle. She had poured maple syrup on her waffle. Annie was absolutely sure the coffee was Maxwell House. She had not expected them to have brand names a hundred years ago.

Strat was having coffee and waffles and bacon and potatoes and biscuits, which seemed like enough.

Devonny was having oatmeal.

Annie had asked for cereal, meaning Rice Krispies or Cheerios, and had received the sturdiest oatmeal in America. Devonny had added brown sugar and raisins and milk to hers, but even when Annie copied her, it was pretty revolting.

Bridget was right there. She looked thinner this morning, and very tired. Annie felt guilty because Bridget was working so hard while Annie was doing absolutely nothing to help, a situation Annie's mother would not have tolerated for one split second, but a houseguest named Anna Sophia Lockwood of course did nothing.

"Would you prefer something other than oatmeal, Miss Lockwood?"

"May I have a piece of toast?" Nobody was having

toast, and perhaps they hadn't gone around singeing their bread in 1895.

But Bridget vanished, down into the bottom of the Mansion where the kitchen was, and came back quickly with thick-cut toast slathered with butter, and adorable little jars of jam to choose from.

Annie was happy. What would they do today? She could hardly wait. She and Strat were communicating by eyelash, by chin tilt and by coffee cup. She memorized him across the table. All this and love too. She could not believe her luck.

Strat kissed the air lightly when nobody else was looking and she kissed back, but her timing was off. Harriett had been looking.

Harriett poked her waffle with her silver fork and seemed to come to a decision.

"I have some news," said Harriett. "I should like to convey this while just the four of us are dining." She took a deep and shaky breath. "Mr. Rowwells proposed marriage to me last night."

Harriett's heart hurt.

It was as if she had laced her stays inside her chest, crushing her very own heart. Please jump up, Strat. Please cry, *No, No, No!* Tell me you love me and you don't want me to do this.

For Harriett did not want to do it.

Mr. Rowwells had turned out to be twelve years older than she. Harriett was unsure of the mechanics of marriage, and would like very much to know how children were produced, but nobody seemed to know that if they weren't married, and if they were married, they seemed determined to keep it a secret.

Whatever it was, you did it in the same bed.

Harriett was pretty sure you did not wear all of your clothing.

She did not want to imagine Mr. Rowwells without all of his clothing. She certainly did not want to imagine herself without all of her clothing while Mr. Rowwells was standing there.

Bridget hurried in with more hot coffee. This was usually Matthew's job. Harriett was terribly sorry for the little babies who had lost their father and chastised herself. She should be thinking of charitable things to do for the widow instead of whimpering because Hiram Stratton, Jr., had a fickle heart.

Harriett had always hoped that her friendship with Strat, their history together, their easy comfort with each other, would override the beauty of houseguests who came and went.

Well, she'd been wrong.

Strat cared only for looks, and he was sitting here throwing kisses to Miss Lockwood as if she, Harriett, did not exist.

She had existed for Mr. Rowwells.

Mr. Rowwells, when they sat together in the library, did not want to hear about books, or college, or education, or even about the games and activities planned for summer.

He wanted to marry her. Now. He was deeply deeply charmed by her, he said. She was perfection.

Harriett tried not to remember that she was also wealth. Immense wealth. Which her husband, when she had one, would control.

But without a husband, was anything worth the bother? You had to be married. And she had been asked, and might not be asked again.

Strat was stunned. Mr. Rowwells! Marry Harriett? It was indecent. Strat had assumed that Aunt Ada had assigned Mr. Rowwells to be kind to Harriett last night. A proposal of marriage went beyond kindness.

He tried to read Harriett's expression. Was she in love with Mr. Rowwells? Did she want this to occur?

Everybody had thought he would eventually marry Harriett. It had sort of been there, expected and ordinary. Not marry Harriett? It was terrible and lonely to think that he would not always have her in his life.

And yet—not marry Harriett? It meant he could think about other girls. About Anna Sophia Lockwood. *Annie.* Strat's heart nearly flew out of his chest.

He was swamped by the scent and touch of her: her hair and lips, her hands and throat. He was possessed by a physical misery he had never dreamed of. It was not joyous to be in love, it was aching and desperate.

I'll ache when Father finds out, he thought. After he whips me for not getting hold of Harriett's money, he'll send me to a factory to work fourteen hours a day. He'll tell people I'm learning the business. He won't mention that he won't be giving me the business after all.

Strat tried to think, but like last night, thinking was a difficult activity.

Suppose he offered Harriett a counter proposal. Suppose he cried out: *No, No, No, No,* Harriet, you and I are destined for each other, I love you dearly, I cannot let you go to another! He would be making his father happy. He might or might not be making Harriett happy.

But he definitely would not be making himself happy.

He knew what his father would say about happiness. It had nothing to do with anything. Money and promises were what counted, and Harriett had the first and Strat should have given the second.

He had to collect himself, behave properly. He could not ignore Harriett to look longingly back at Annie, nor rip Annie's clothing off, which was the utterly indecent thought that kept coming into his mind and which he kept having to tromp down.

He floundered, wanting to do the right thing for Harriett, of whom he was very fond, and the right thing for himself, but it was too quick. Harriett had shown poor manners in springing this. People needed to be prepared, and she should have had Aunt Ada tell them privately so they could think of the proper things to say.

Should he offer congratulations? But who could be happy about the prospect of a life with Mr. Rowwells? Besides, the event that was going to happen along with

Harriett's marriage to Mr. Rowwells was his own execution.

Devonny said, "That's disgusting, Harriett. He's disgusting. He's old and disgusting."

They all giggled hysterically, but Harriett's giggles turned to tears and she excused herself, holding her big white linen napkin to her face, and ran back into the house and up the great stairs to her room.

"Strat, you pitiful excuse for a man," said his sister. "You should have told her you love her and you don't want her to marry Mr. Rowwells. What if she says *yes?* Then where will you be?"

Strat knew where he would be.

With Annie.

Surely, love this strong was meant to be. Surely no parent would stand in the way. Surely even Strat's father would understand that this was not ordinary, his love for Miss Lockwood, and it was providence that Mr. Rowwells had stepped in to take care of Harriett.

Oh, the brutal necessity of marriage. Poor poor Harriett! Poor Florinda. Poor those other three wives. Poor Ada, who'd had no marriage. And maybe, just maybe, poor Miss Bartten, who wanted it so badly she was willing to destroy a marriage to get her own.

And me, thought Annie Lockwood, straddling time. What am I destroying? Will I end up with a marriage? All I wanted was a summer romance.

She did not want to think about any of this. For none of this was love and romance: it was power. I have the most power, she thought. It makes me the father, the man in the story.

She refused to have heavy thoughts. It was a perfect morning with a perfect boy. She studied the perfect embroidery on the glossily starched linen napkins.

A servant approached uneasily. "Sir?" he said to Strat.

Annie loved how they called each other Sir and Mister and Miss.

Strat raised his eyebrows.

"The police are here once more, sir, and wish to converse with the young people about last night. Matthew's unfortunate accident, sir."

Prickliness settled over Annie, as if in her own time she had read about this, and knew the ending, and the ending was terrible and wrong. She forgot the melodrama of Harriett's flight.

Was I sent here to change the ending? But if that's the case, I should remember more clearly, I should know what to do next.

She was afraid of Time now, and what it could do and where it could take you, and the lies it could tell. It was time to face something. Police. Death. Murder. Stairs. Time.

Strat escorted them into the library, Devonny on one arm and Annie on the other.

The library was Victorian decorating at its darkest and most frightening. The high ceilings were crossed by blackly carved beams. The walls were covered with books, the sort whose leather bindings match. The books sagged and were dusty and the room stank of cigars and pipes. Dried flowers dropped little gray leaves beneath them. Drapes obliterated the windows, and huge paintings with gold frames as swollen as disease hung too high to see. Carpets were piled on carpets, and the pillars that divided the shelves were carved with mouths: open jaws, the jaws of monsters and trolls.

Mr. Stratton's immense bulk was tightly wrapped in yet another dark suit, with vest and jacket and silk scarf. Mr. Rowwells was his likeness: younger, not so corpulent, but creepily similar. The hag chaperon stood in a corner, as if made for corners.

She was the one Annie most didn't want to think about. Aunt Ada was wreckage, and yet also power.

The police were apologetic and unsure. Next to Mr. Rowwells and Mr. Stratton, they were thin and pale and badly dressed. Mr. Stratton had done everything in his power to intimidate them, and he had done well, but he had not entirely succeeded. They had returned.

Mr. Rowwells tamped his pipe. A faint scent of apples and autumn came from the tobacco. His face was overweight: drooping jowls and heavy hanging eyelids. How could Harriett want to get near him, let alone get married?

I'm playing games, thought Annie, but this is Harriett's life.

She tried to figure out how much of this was a game, and how much was real. Swiftly and sickeningly, it went all too real.

"That's her!" Mr. Rowwells jabbed a thick fat finger

at Annie. His fleshy lips pulled back from his teeth and his nicotine-stained fingers spread to grab her. The heavy lids peeled back from bulging eyes. "She's the one who pushed Matthew!" he shouted. "I saw her!" His eyes were like the stair gargoyles, bloodstained.

The room tilted and fell beneath Annie's feet.

Elegantly costumed people rotated like dressed mannequins, and the faces locked eyes on her.

What do they see? Do they see the witch that Bridget saw? Will they hang me? How do I explain traveling through time?

"Get her!" shouted Mr. Rowwells.

They advanced like a lynch mob.

Her own long skirt was eager to trip her. It grabbed her ankles so they didn't have to. She seized the cloth in her hands and whipped around to race out of the library, but Strat hung onto her. She ripped herself free of him. *I wasn't sent to make things right, I was sent to take the blame. I fell through time in order to be punished for a murder I didn't commit.*

Annie flew through the Great Hall, slipping on the black and white squares. Her frenzy was carrying her faster than theirs, or perhaps they did not dream that a lady could conduct herself like this. They were shouting, but not running. Strat was close behind but she made it out the door.

She took a desperate look toward the village, to see if 1995 lay there, with its bridges and turnpikes and cars.

It didn't.

Being outside won't save me, she thought. Only

time will save me. But I don't know how I got here, so I don't know how to go back.

She ran.

Strat ran after her.

"Annie! Miss Lockwood! Stop!"

She ducked through an opening in the stone walls surrounding the garden. If she remembered it right from childhood picnics, there should be a path to the stables.

Strat caught up. He wrapped both arms around her, like a prison.

But it was not simply a path to the stables. It was a path through time. She had been running the right way.

She could hear the noise of Strat's century, the cries of the household, the whinny of a horse, but she could also hear her own. Radios and the honk of a horn and the grinding of combustion engines.

Although it had never happened to her before, and possibly never happened to anyone else before, she knew that one step forward and she would be gone.

Strat's embrace softened. He too wore morning dress, as if for a senior prom: black suit, white shirt, the cut of his trousers and the fall of his hair from his century and not hers. Oh, how she adored him!

I love him. How could I have thought he was a toy? He's so wonderfully real. *I'm* the one who isn't real!

"I love you," said Strat.

Words half formed and were half there, just as she was now half formed and half there. *I want to stay,* she tried to tell him, *I love you, but I don't want to be hung for somebody's murder! Last night, Strat, you even asked if I could get out if I had to. I have to, Strat.*

She tried to kiss him, but she possessed no muscles. She was on both sides of time, and on neither.

"Please," whispered Strat. "Choose me."

Was that true? Was it her choice? Had she chosen to travel? Or had it been chosen for her?

I will always choose you! she cried.

But choice was not hers after all. He was going, or she was going, whichever way time spun.

The tunnel of time swallowed her.

"It wasn't you he was pointing at!" yelled Strat. His words blew from his mouth like wind. "It was the maid! It was Bridget! Just a fight between servants!"

I love you, Strat, she cried, but there was no sound, for she wasn't there anymore.

Strat threw all her names after her, as if one would surely catch and hold. "Stay, Annie! Anna Sophia! Miss Lockwood!"

A nightmare of history flew through her head and shot past her eyes.

Strat cried out once more, but she could not quite hear him, and the sound turned into quarreling seagulls and there she was, on a bright and beautiful morning, alone on the shabby grounds of a teetering old building soon to be torn down.

CHAPTER 8

Bodies surrounded Bridget, each tightly cased in heavy waistcoats or rigid corsets. Each chest filled with air and fury and took up more space and pressed harder against her. Beyond the flesh and cloth, the jaws of leering gargoyles gaped back. The bodies closed in on her like a living noose. She clung to her apron as if it could protect her life the way it protected her dress. "No," sobbed Bridget. "I never. It isn't true! May Jesus, Mary and Joseph—"

"Don't start with your Catholic noises, miss," said Mr. Stratton senior. He loomed over her, his great girth in its satiny waistcoat brushing against her white apron.

Bridget's head pounded. She could not even begin to think about Miss Lockwood and young Mr. Stratton racing out of the house like hound dogs. "But, sir, Mr. Rowwells is not telling the truth. He could not have seen me push Matthew. I did no such thing! Why would I ever?"

"Ah, but I think you would, Bridget," said Walker Walkley, with his fine mouth and sweet eyes. He had not joined the living noose, but stood like a portrait of himself, casually displayed against the scarlet leather bindings of a long row of books. "When you followed me into my room last night, Bridget, and tried to force your affections upon me, and when I, a gentleman, refused you, did you not spit upon me? Did you not threaten me? Did you not say that if you had a chance, *you would shove me down the stairs like Matthew?*"

Everybody in the room gasped, a chorus of horror.

"I spit on you," said Bridget, "because *you—*"

"A threat, I may point out," said Walker Walkley smoothly, talking now to the police, so that nobody listened to the end of Bridget's sentence, "only hours after Matthew was found dead on the stairs."

Aunt Ada smiled inside her toothless mouth. Her lips folded down like pillowcases. "Wicked, shameless, lying creature," said Ada. "You killed Matthew!" Ada stepped away from Bridget. As if it were a dance step— perhaps the dance to a hanging—all the ladies and gentlemen stepped back. "To think, Hiram," said Ada, "that after she killed Matthew, she attended to Miss Devonny!"

"I trusted my daughter in her sleep to a murderer," said Hiram Stratton. He turned to the police. "Thank you for coming. I was incorrect to try to dissuade you from your duty. I am most grateful for your persistence. Had you not returned for more questions, I should never have realized what kind of person I was harboring on my staff."

An officer on each side of her gripped her arms above the elbow, tightly, as if she were some sort of animal about to be branded.

"Miss Devonny," whispered Bridget. "Please. You know I didn't." Had not Bridget waited on Miss Devonny all these months? Brushed her hair, tended her in her bath, told her stories of Ireland, listened to Devonny's stories of stepmothers?

But Miss Devonny did not answer. In fact, she turned her face from Bridget's, believing that what she did not see, she need not think about. Devonny would take the word of a gentleman before she ever considered the word of a serving girl.

I have no friends, thought Bridget. And Jeb . . . will he come to the aid of an Irish Catholic accused of murder?

"Take her away," said Mr. Stratton to the police.

"No!" shrieked Bridget. "Miss Devonny! You know I wouldn't do any such thing! Don't let them say things like this about me! It was Mr. Walkley who tried to yank my dress right off!"

"It just goes to show," said Mr. Stratton, mildly, for Bridget was no longer of consequence, "that no immigrant can be trusted. We shouldn't have accepted that Statue of Liberty, with that sentimental poem about taking in the huddled masses. They're nothing but murderers carrying disease."

Walker Walkley put his arms around Devonny,

turning her head gently against his chest, to protect her from the sight.

"Thank goodness my fiancée is not here," said Mr. Rowwells. "I demand that there be no discussion of this in front of Miss Harriett. She is too delicate to be apprised of the fact that the very maid who attended her is a murderess."

The police removed Bridget as they might remove a roadblock; she was a thing. No one in the library thought of her again. The question now was far greater than Bridget or Matthew. The question now was money. Harriett's money.

"Fiancée?" said Mr. Stratton dangerously. "What are you talking about, Rowwells? Where is my son? Ada, pry him away from that crazy girl and get him in here. You are not, Mr. Rowwells, affianced to Harriett Ranleigh."

Mortar had fallen from the stone pillar that once supported the porte cochere. Rotted shingles had peeled away and paint was long gone from the trim. Every window was boarded and a thick chain sealed the great doors.

The air felt empty, as if Annie were alone in the world. Sounds were faint, as if they had happened earlier, and were only echoes.

She shivered in the damp crawling shade of the Mansion. In the turnaround lay hamburger wrappers, soda cans and an old bent beach chair, its vinyl straps torn and flapping. Annie's century at its ugliest.

How could a thing so vivid have been only in her mind, nothing but electrical charges gone wild? Could Strat have been just a twitch of her eyelid in sleep?

No, she thought, he was Strat, my Strat, and I have lost him. Forever. If it is 1995, then he is dead. To me and to the world.

She fell kneeling onto the grass and the one syllable of his name seemed to tear out of her throat with enough force to cross time. *Strat!*

Perhaps the syllable did, but Annie didn't.

And love. Love couldn't cross time either. Love was gone. Only loss remained.

She sobbed, but tears have never changed history.

Annie Lockwood got on her bike.

It had not gone a hundred years with her. Nothing had gone a hundred years with her. Because she hadn't gone a hundred years. Of course it had been a dream; what else could time travel be but a dream?

She felt thick and heavy and stupid.

It was hard to sit on the bike, hard to find the pedals. At the top of the steep drive, she waited for the horses, but of course there was neither horse nor carriage. Against the old stone walls, leaves were mounded in rotting piles, for the gardeners who had swept were long gone.

She tightened her hands on the brakes and went slowly down the Great Hill. No golf course at the bottom, but picnic grounds: a hundred wooden tables spread unevenly over high meadowy grass.

Annie pushed her feet down alternately. It seemed like a very foreign skill, one that she had seen, but never done herself. The same, but oh, so different road she and Strat had followed. When? A hundred years ago? Hours ago? Or not at all?

She rode away from the silence and death of the old Mansion, into the racket and life of the public beach.

Hundreds—perhaps thousands—of people were enjoying the Stratton estate on this hot and sunny day in June. Bathing suits and Bermuda shorts, beach towels and suntan lotion, Cokes and bologna sandwiches. Lifeguards and tennis courts and hot dog concessions. Station wagons and BMWs and Jeeps and convertibles.

Her ears were filled by rushing noise, waterfalls in her head, as if she had swum too long underwater.

Where did time go, when you traveled down it?

Was it today or tomorrow? Should she ask? *Excuse me, is this the day school ended, or the day after? I need to know if time went on without me or just sat here waiting for me to get back.*

Annie Lockwood pedaled on, as exhausted as if she had traveled a hundred years.

"And did you," said Mr. Stratton, "plight your troth to Mr. Rowwells?"

How yellow he seemed, his teeth tobacco-stained and his face jaundiced. His beard bristled at Harriett, and the tips of his huge mustache sagged into the words he spat at her. He was her guardian, the one who protected her from life, but it was not Harriett's welfare he cared about; it was his.

Harriett could not bear to look at Mr. Rowwells, who was less heavy and hairy only because he was younger than Mr. Stratton, and hadn't had time to acquire as much belly and beard. But he would, and Harriett would be his wife while he did it. Mr. Rowwells' ugly bristly face would brush up against hers and she could never turn away.

She had said yes when he asked for her hand, and had let her hand rest in his, sealing the agreement.

A short word. An easy word.

A dangerous, complete word. *Yes.*

No! shrieked Harriett's heart. No, no, no, no, no, no, no! I cannot marry this man. I cannot do with him whatever it is that married people do.

But she had said that word, that little word yes, and it was a promise, and promises could not be broken. Oh, if she actually stood in the aisle in front of the altar and said, "No," the rector at the Episcopal church would not force her to go through with the ceremony. But the shame and the scandal would be worse than the marriage.

Nobody would associate with her. She would have no friends.

She tried to imagine being friends with Mr. Rowwells the way she was friends with Strat. Oh, Strat, Strat, I love you so! Where did Miss Lockwood come from and why did you fall in love with her?

Mr. Stratton moved closer. She felt burned by the smoking anger of her guardian. His waistcoat slithered against the silk jacket lining, and the chain of his pocket watch bounced against the rolls of his flesh. I will be chained by marriage, thought Harriett, just as Bridget is now chained in jail. Perhaps they are the same thing: jail and marriage to someone you don't like.

"Did you," said Mr. Stratton once more, his fury darkening the room, "accept the marriage proposal of Clarence Rowwells?"

I could lie, thought Harriett. I could say I listened to Mr. Rowwells' proposal and didn't respond. But I did respond. I said yes.

I am a lady, and ladies give their word, and never break it.

"I said yes," said Harriet. Something in her died, seeing her future. College? What was that? She would never know. What about the lovely wedding Devonny had planned? What about the laughing honeymoon?

Mr. Stratton's fist slammed down with the force of a steam piston. He did not hit her. He hit the back of the leather chair, and then he hit it a second time, and a third. His cigar-thick fingers stayed in a yellow fist that he swung toward Aunt Ada. "Where were you when this was taking place?" he hissed, his boiler steam building to explosion. "Why do you think I have housed you all these years? For my entertainment, Ada?"

Ada did not flinch. Mr. Rowwells did not tremble. They seemed almost a pair, and Harriett suddenly knew that not only would she be married to Mr. Rowwells, she would never be free of Ada; they would jointly own her.

"I was attempting to corral young Mr. Stratton,"

said Ada venomously. "He went flying after his little tramp, Hiram." Ada did not, as she usually did, put a hand up to hide her toothless condition. Her smile was hideous and wet. "Like father, like son, Hiram. Young Mr. Stratton thinks only of the flesh of beautiful girls."

I am not beautiful, thought Harriett. All my life I will look into mirrors and see a plain woman. I don't love Strat any less. I'm not even mad at him. I am the fool who said yes. I could have said no, and I didn't, because at the moment I thought any marriage was better than no marriage.

I love everything about Strat. I will always love everything about him. "You may place no blame on Strat," said Harriett quietly. "I am a woman of twenty who knows her own mind. I did consent to the proposal of marriage from Mr. Rowwells."

There could be no more argument.

She could never retrieve those words.

Even if Strat were to forget Miss Lockwood, and repent of his ways, and want Harriett back, it could never happen now.

For Harriett Ranleigh had given her word.

Bridget stood very still in the middle of the cell. Perhaps if she did not move, not ever again in this life, the filth and horror would not touch her. The cell was in a windowless cellar, and even though it was noon, no light entered the hole into which she had been shoved.

The scrabbling noises were rats. When she was too

tired to stand she would have to lie down among them.

She thought of the little room she shared with two kitchen maids, the thin mattress on the iron cot, the freshly ironed heavy white sheets, cotton blankets, and breeze off the ocean. She thought of the breakfast she had not yet had, for the family must be served first. She thought of the money wrapped in a handkerchief and saved so carefully for her future.

Bridget was not romantic. She knew better. Life was harsh, and she'd been foolish to think that would change. Jeb would be humiliated that he'd ever been seen in her presence. He'd believe the stories about her because they were told by gentlemen. Would Mr. Walkley and Mr. Rowwells lie?

No, and how did they make fortunes? Being kind? No. By putting people like me in places like this.

I will not cry, Bridget said to herself.

But she cried, and it was not over Jeb, or the lost hopes for her life, or even the rats, but because Miss Devonny had not said a word in her defense.

"Well, Walker Walkley," she said to the rats, "you are a rat if there ever was one. You seized your chance for revenge. And now I surely would shove you down the stairs if I could ever get you to the top of one. As for Miss Devonny, she'll probably marry you. And if that's the case, she'll get what she deserves. A rat."

So much traffic!

Everybody who owned a car had decided to circle

the old Stratton roads, make sure the ocean was still there, get a glimpse of summer to come.

Annie biked on the shoulder to avoid being hit. Just because they were sight-seeing did not mean anybody drove slowly or carefully. The road wound around two huge horse chestnut trees on which kids had been carving initials for generations. From this distance, the Mansion had kept its aura. The towers still glistened in the sun. The great veranda, with its views of shore and beach, still looked down on her.

She was blinded by tears, a rush of emotion so strong she could not believe it came from dreams on the sand. Oh, Strat! You were real, I know you were! I loved you, I know I did!

A horn blared so hard and close that Annie all but rode her bike right into a battered, rusted-out old van, every window open, dripping with the faces of teenagers she didn't know. They were laughing and pointing at her, their fingers too sharp and their mouths too wide. "Nice dress!" they yelled sarcastically. "Where's the party? What's your problem, girl?"

She was wearing the morning gown. A simple dress by the standards of Harriett and Devonny, but in 1995—!

She jerked the bike off the road and down a dirt footpath into the holly gardens, where green-spiked walls hid her. The van honked several more times but moved on without pursuing her. People didn't like to get out of their cars, even at the beach.

Long rows of tiny hand-sewn pleats. Long bands of

delicate gauzy lace. Beneath them, the ribs of her corset.

I was there. It happened. This is the dress that Bridget put me into! This is the—

Bridget!

A century too late, a full hundred years too late, she heard Strat's voice, and understood. It was Bridget that Mr. Rowwells had accused, not Miss Lockwood.

"Oh, no!" she cried out loud, as if the Strattons were there to hear her. "But I know what happened. I have to go back!"

I wasn't listening to Strat. Why don't I ever listen? What's the matter with me? I thought only of myself. I panicked. I was afraid of 1895. Afraid of what they could do to me, without my family, without my own world. I found an opening and I fled.

They will do it to Bridget.

Even the nicest people had spoken cruelly of the Irish. They would believe anything of an Irish maid. Bridget as murderer was easier than the truth, so they would let it stand.

How vividly now Annie remembered the fury with which Matthew's life had been taken; *had* to be taken; for Matthew was the one who could not tell what he had learned.

Annie could not hurry in the ridiculous morning gown. She peeled it off and stood in the underdress. Annie was still overdressed for the beach, though Harriett and Devonny would have fainted before appearing in public in an undergarment.

Her bookbag was still strapped to the bike. She

wadded up the morning gown, shoved it in with the gum wrappers and broken pencils and extra nickels, and leaped back on. "I'm coming, Bridget!" she yelled.

But how will I do it? What wand or witch took me through when I fell? What magic stone or cry of the heart? Where exactly was I standing, and what exactly was I thinking and touching?

I got in, she said to herself, and I came out, so I can go back. I have to.

But it was no magic stone or glass that appeared in front of Annie.

It was a police car, very 1995, its driver very angry, and its purpose very clear.

They had finished the short subject of where Miss Lockwood had gone. Harriett and Devonny were unwilling to accept Strat's idea that she had gone to another century.

The young people were back on the veranda, as if nothing had happened. As if no lives had been changed. Mr. Rowwells had cornered Mr. Stratton in his library, and forced a discussion of Harriett's property. Without her present, of course. Any hope that Mr. Rowwells was actually fond of her was gone.

Harriett secured her morning hat to her hair with her favorite hat pin, which was six inches long with a pearl tip. She need not worry that Strat would see she was close to tears. Strat was close to tears himself.

For a while, nothing was heard but the stirring of coffee.

When Aunt Ada joined them, it seemed unlikely that the subject of century changes would come up again.

Besides, Devonny was more interested in Matthew and Bridget than in broken hearts. "Do you really think Bridget approached Walk like that?" said Devonny. "Bridget was shy with Jeb. She wanted to be a lady. She was always copying my behavior."

"Do not contradict Mr. Walkley's statement," said Aunt Ada sharply. "He has explained what Bridget did and that is that. Where are your manners?"

"I'm worried about Bridget," said Devonny. "What will happen to her?"

"There are prisons for women," said Aunt Ada. "I expect she'll be locked up forever. Or hanged. It's better to hang them. Otherwise they have to be fed for decades."

"I should have spoken up," said Devonny, knotting her skirt between her fingers. Aunt Ada yanked Devonny's fingers up and glared at her for fidgeting. "I should have insisted on more proof," said Devonny.

"Mind your posture," snapped Ada, smartly whacking the center of Devonny's back.

Devonny straightened. I hate you, she thought, and I like Bridget. I've heard rumors about Walker Walkley. He's supposed to be very loose and free with the maids in his household. If Bridget came to his room and offered herself, would he say no?

Devonny wondered what it meant, for a girl to offer herself. What exactly did they do next? Was it something she wanted to know? Yes. Desperately.

I believe, Devonny said to herself, that Walker Walkley knows, and likes it, and he would laugh and say yes.

So Walk is lying that Bridget tried to force herself on him. It was probably the other way around. Therefore Walker is also lying that she threatened him.

And if I don't believe that Bridget accosted Walk, I also don't believe Bridget accosted Matthew. And I still don't know to whom Matthew was bringing the sherry.

Devonny was angry with herself for thinking too slowly. Why had she not brought this up when Bridget and the police were there? Why must she think things out hours later, possibly too many hours later to fix the situation?

But even if I don't believe Walk, she remembered, there is Mr. Rowwells. He saw Bridget push Matthew. *He* wouldn't lie. You couldn't have *two* gentlemen lying!

Devonny thought of Harriett marrying Mr. Rowwells instead of Strat. It was disgusting. Devonny didn't even want to be in the wedding party now. How would they have a good time? What difference would the world's loveliest dress make, if you were marrying Clarence Rowwells? As for Strat, mooning over some creature he claimed lived in another world—he was worthless!

Why had Miss Lockwood run away? When that finger had pointed, why had she thought it pointed at her?

But Mr. Rowwells could not have confused Miss Lockwood, who would have been bare-legged and hatless at the time of Matthew's murder, with Bridget in her big white starched apron.

"She says people have orange juice every morning," Strat offered.

Devonny got oranges in her Christmas stockings, because they were so unusual and special. "Strat," said his sister, "unless you want my coffee in your face, tell the truth."

"That's what she said."

"Nobody cares what she said," Devonny told him. "We care where she went, and where *you* were back when we needed you in the library, and who she is, anyhow."

"I was looking for her," he said miserably. "I looked everywhere."

When he'd caught her, hidden in the shade of dancing trees, she'd turned with strange, slowed-down gestures, as if she had miles to go. Her hair had been piled so enticingly, her eyes so large and warm, her pretty lips half open.

And then, he'd lost sight of her. She wavered, becoming a reflection of herself. She literally slipped between his fingers. He was holding her gown, and then he wasn't. He'd had a strand of her hair, and then he didn't.

And then nothing of her had been present.

Just Strat and the soft morning air.

When he stopped shouting, he tried whispering, as if her vanishing were a secret, and he could pull her out. "Annie! Anna Sophia! Miss Lockwood." And then, louder, achingly, "Annie! Annie!"

She had not come. She was not there.

The lump in his throat persisted. Perhaps he was getting diphtheria. He would rather have a fatal disease than a fatal love. At least people would be on his side. If he died of not having Miss Lockwood, his family would simply be scornful.

He tried to laugh at himself, in love with a person who did not exist, but nothing was funny. His chest ached along with his throat, and his eyes blistered.

He looked up and saw his sister's disgust and Harriett's sorrow. Her eyes too were blistered with pain. Strat wanted to hold Harriett's hands, tell her he was sorry that he had failed her, that he was worthless, that he—

But Mr. Rowwells arrived, and claimed his property, and Harriett Ranleigh rose obediently in the presence of her future husband and left.

CHAPTER 9

Policemen a hundred years ago had come in a high black carriage, worn no weapons, been nervous and unsure. The officer who got out of this gray Crown Victoria with its whirling blue lights was a man in charge. He was middle-aged, overweight and very angry. "Annie Lockwood?" he said grimly.

She didn't need to ask if time had gone on without her. It definitely had.

"Just where have you been, young lady? There has been a search organized for you since late last night."

"Please," said Annie, trying desperately to span her two centuries and her two problems. "I can't talk to you now. I have to get back to—well, you see, a hundred years ago—"

He popped the trunk and stuck her bike in with his rescue kit and blanket. "The beach closed last night at ten o'clock. We combed the sand, we searched the breakwaters. We had the Mansion opened up, we walked through every room, including the most dangerous, to see if you'd fallen through a floor. We've questioned each and every car to enter Stratton Point this morning, in case they were here yesterday and saw something."

Annie swallowed.

"How much cop time do you think you wasted, young lady?"

"I'm sorry."

"How much sleep do you think your mom or dad got last night?"

She began to cry.

"Your mother brought your school pictures for us to show around. But we were right. You just went off, without letting anybody know where or why, the way stupid thoughtless teenagers do." He opened the front door roughly, as if he would like to treat her that roughly, but he didn't, and Annie got in.

"So you were here all the time," he said. "Ignored the sirens? Ignored everybody calling your name? Ignored the flashlights and the searchers? Would you like to know what I think of kids like you?"

She knew already. And he was right. Kids like that were worthless.

Her mind framed answers she didn't dare say aloud: I wasn't worthless! I fell through time. I really wasn't here. I didn't hide from you. I didn't mean for you to waste all those cop hours.

At the very same moment that a search party had been flashing its beams into the dark and moldering corners of an unoccupied ballroom, she had been dancing with Strat on its beautifully polished floor.

"Who was with you?" said the cop. "Is he still here?"

He was right about the pronoun: it had certainly been a boy. But explain Strat? When even Annie did not know whether he was still here? Or always here? Or never here?

And what about Bridget? Time went on. The policeman had just made that clear. So time was also going on a hundred years ago, and whatever was happening to Bridget was happening now.

"I'm sorry," she said, trying not to sob out loud. "I'm sorry you had to waste time. I guess I—um—fell asleep on the sand."

Like he believed that.

He not only took her home, he held her arm going up to the front door, as if she were a prisoner. She was afraid of him, and yet she was only going home. What was Bridget feeling, who might be hung? Did they have fair trials back then? Who would speak for Bridget?

"Where have you been?" screamed her father, jerking her into the house. He was shaking. He tried to thank the policeman, but he was so collapsed with exhaustion and relief and fury that he couldn't pull it off.

"We've called every friend you ever had looking for you!" shrieked her mother. She was trembling.

"I'm sorry," said Annie lamely. Around her were the television and stereo, stacks of tapes for the VCR, ice maker clunking out cubes, dishwasher whining, her brother, Tod, sipping a Coke, wearing a rock star T-shirt . . . How was Annie supposed to tell where she had been?

I changed centuries, I witnessed a murder, I fell in love. Right.

"You better have a good excuse for this," said her mother, voice raw.

"There is no excuse good enough for this," said her father.

Annie shivered in the white undergown and her mother's eyes suddenly focused on its hand-sewn pleats and lace. Mom knew Annie's wardrobe, knew the dress she'd set out in yesterday morning, knew that not only did Annie not own a dress like this, but nobody anywhere owned a dress like this.

But her mother did not comment on the dress.

"I just fell asleep on the sand," said Annie finally. "I'm sorry. I'm so sorry. It was so hot out, and I was exhausted from the end of school, and I went down to the far end of the beach where all the rocks are and you can't swim, and nobody even picnics, so I could be alone, and I fell asleep. I'm really really sorry. I just didn't wake up. It's been a very stressful year and I guess I slept it off."

The cop shook his head, then shook hands with her father and left.

"I'm so sorry," Annie said once more. And she *was* sorry; sorry they'd been scared, sorry she wasn't still with Strat, sorry she couldn't save Bridget, sorry, sorry, sorry.

She burst into tears, Mom burst into tears, and

they hugged each other. Mom was going to accept this excuse. Perhaps Mom had had so much practice accepting Dad's thin excuses that thin was good now; she was used to thin. Even when Mom's fingernails, bitten and broken from the shock of a lost daughter, touched the work-of-art gown, Mom asked no questions.

Dad, however, was too much of an expert at thin excuses. He recognized thin when he saw it.

Tod, of course, being her brother, knew perfectly well she was lying like a rug. These, in fact, were the words he mouthed from behind Mom and Dad. *Lying like a rug,* he shaped.

"I feel like thrashing you," yelled her father, circling the furniture to prevent himself from doing just that. "Putting us through last night. Scaring your mother and me like this."

"I'm sorry," she said again.

"You are grounded! No boyfriend, no beach, no bike, no car, no nothing. You'll have a great summer, the way you've started off."

If there was one thing Annie hadn't been, it was "grounded." She'd been airborne. Century-borne. Time-borne.

And now she was stuck in a conversation they might repeat forever, Dad shrieking, Annie being sorry.

"Let it go, David," said Mom finally. "She's fine. Nothing really happened. Let's not ruin the weekend."

It isn't so much that she accepts thin excuses, thought Annie. Mom just plain doesn't want to know the truth. Because what if the truth is ugly? Or immoral? Mom prefers ignorance.

"I want to know what really happened," said Dad fiercely. He brushed his wife aside as if she were clothes in a closet.

It was that brush that did it for Annie. That physical sweep of the arm, getting rid of the annoying female opinion. She could see a whole long century of men brushing their wives aside.

Annie had never thought of telling her father off. She and Tod, without ever talking about it, had known that they would maintain silence, even between themselves, on the subject of Dad and Miss Bartten.

But the flight between centuries upset her master plan. The loss of Strat and the failure to save Bridget loosened her defenses. A year of pretending exploded in the Lockwoods' faces.

Annie said from between gritted teeth, "You do, huh? You want to tell Mom what really happens when *you're* not where you're supposed to be? You want to tell Mom about Miss Bartten? You want to tell Mom who's with *you* when *you* fall asleep on the sand?"

Her father's face drained of color. He ceased to breathe.

Her brother Tod froze, cake halfway to his mouth.

Annie was holding her breath, too, from rage and fright.

But somebody was breathing, loud, rasping, desperate breathing.

Mom.

Mom, who had never wanted to know, never

wanted to acknowledge what was happening to her life—Mom knew now.

For better or for worse, in her wisdom, or in her total lack of wisdom, Annie had made her see.

Fat white pillars stood beneath a sky-blue ceiling. Trellises supported morning glories bluer than the sky. The remaining houseguests strolled the grounds, eager for a most difficult weekend to close. The boys could not put together a ball game, there were too few of them, and they were worried about Strat. His father had once, at immense cost to himself, shut down a railroad spur forever rather than have union workers tell him what to do. What would Mr. Stratton do to his son?

Strat had disobeyed, and hardly even knew it. Mind and body clouded by his missing Anna Sophia, he was wandering around the estate stroking things and muttering to himself. Strat was saying even now that he wished he'd thought to bring out the camera. "I have a new tripod," he said miserably. "I should have taken her photograph." He frowned a little. "Do you suppose she would have photographed? Would her picture have come out?"

"Strat!" yelled Devonny. "She was there! She was real! She wore Harriett's clothes, Bridget brushed her hair, she ate her toast, she existed! Of course she would photograph!"

Strat sighed hugely.

"She's here somewhere," said Devonny. "She can't

get off the estate without going by the gatehouse. Of course, the woods are deep, and perhaps she crept in there, but I refuse to believe she's living off berries. She'll be back, but this time she'll claim to be a desperate orphan."

Harriett wore a hat with heavy veiling, not to ward off the sun but to hide her red eyes and trembling mouth. She slipped away from the topics of murder and missing girls, and walked down the hill and across the golf course to the sand.

Once Harriett had loved collecting sand jewels. Dry starfish and gold shells and sand-washed mermaids' tears.

Behind the veil, real tears washed her face. The mermaids' tears rested soft and warm in her palm, as if tears, like marriage, lasted forever.

"You had to say something, didn't you?" shouted Tod. "You couldn't just wait for it to end by itself, could you? You had to start things!"

"I didn't start anything! Dad started it."

"It was going to work out, Annie," said Tod, "it was going to end, and they would've stayed married."

Tod and Annie spent a hideous afternoon hiding in the hall, trying to overhear Mom and Dad. The word divorce was not used. Tod was hanging on to that. He wanted his family so much he could have killed his sister for starting this, and had to remind himself that a boy who wanted his family intact could not begin by killing his sister.

Mom used few words. She used tissues, and kept walking between window and computer, as if a view or a keyboard would supply answers.

Dad told the truth. He told more of it than even Tod or Annie had dreamed of. But he didn't want a divorce either. He wanted it all. He wanted them both.

What is this? thought Tod. A hundred years ago when men had mistresses? It doesn't work in 1995, Dad. Grow up.

Eventually their mother invited the children to be part of the discussion. Tod said he was fine, thanks, he didn't really—

"Come here," said Mom, her voice as heavy as Stonehenge.

They went there.

"Sit," said Mom, like a dog trainer.

They sat.

"You knew?" she said.

They nodded.

"How long?" she said.

They shrugged.

"A long time then," she said. She looked for another long time at her husband and then she got up and went to her room.

Dad looked mutinously at his daughter, as if he intended to blame her for this, and Annie said, "Dad. Don't even think for one minute about blaming me."

Dad fished in his pocket for his car keys. He would just get into his car and drive away. That was the good thing about 1995: you could always drive away. What would Harriett's life, or Bridget's, be like if either girl could just get in her car and drive away?

I do deserve blame, thought Annie. When in doubt, shut up. That's the rule. I smashed it. Maybe I smashed the whole family.

She saw her two worlds at once, then, like transparencies for an overhead projector lying on top of each other.

She had smashed another family too.

She had smashed Harriett. Damaged Strat. Interfered with lives that had been fine without her.

The convenient knock on the door was Sean, interrupting them.

Dad escaped. "Don't forget you're grounded," he threw over his shoulder. "And you'd better have something nice to say to Sean too. He's been as worried about you as we were."

"Sean? Worried about *me*?" she said in disbelief, and opened the door.

Sean stormed in as if he owned Annie Lockwood. "Well?" he yelled. "You better have one good excuse, ASL. Just where were you last night?"

CHAPTER 10

"What is the matter with you?" bellowed Mr. Stratton. "I said that the topic of Matthew was closed!" How well he resembled the dark and horrid carvings in his own library.

"Bridget did not push Matthew, Hiram," said Florinda. "She was with me in the garden. She was holding my parasol. I am on my way to the village to get her out of that jail."

If the trees had walked over to join the conversation, Hiram Stratton could not have been more amazed. Florinda talking back? To him?

"Oh, Florinda, I'm so glad!" cried Devonny. "I'll go with you. I should have spoken up for her. I knew it at the time, and I failed her in her hour of need."

"No daughter and no wife of mine will approach a jail," said Mr. Stratton. He positioned himself in front of Devonny and Florinda, but they were outdoors, with room to maneuver, and Florinda simply walked around him to the carriage.

"We must," said Florinda. "We have a responsibility to Bridget. I cannot imagine what Mr. Rowwells saw, but it was not Bridget."

"Florinda, you know how confused you become in too much sun. You have the time amiss," said Aunt Ada.

Way down on the beach, Mr. Rowwells caught up to Harriett. It seemed to Devonny that if Harriett ever needed Ada as a chaperon it was now.

"Ada, this is my household," said Florinda. "I do not have the time amiss, and Bridget could not have pushed Matthew."

"Do not contradict me," said Ada.

Hiram Stratton, Sr., stared back and forth between the two women as if learning tennis by watching the ball. What had happened to his neatly ordered household?

"It is you, Ada," said Florinda, "who is daring to contradict me. Whose home is this?"

Devonny was delighted. Florinda might have a use after all. Mean and nasty Ada would be removed, while Florinda would save people, and even take care of Matthew's babies.

Mr. Stratton's anger smoked once more, and Strat tensed. His father had never struck Devonny or Florinda that Strat knew of, but this was striking posture. A blow from such a man could loosen teeth or break a jaw.

Strat moved casually between his father and the ladies.

"We wouldn't be faced with anything, Devonny," Mr. Stratton spat out, "except that you interfered where you have no right even to have thoughts."

His father brushed Strat aside, and advanced on Devonny.

"Father, I do have the right to have thoughts," she said nervously. She did not move back.

Florinda removed a hat pin from the veiling of her immense hat, and admired the glitter of the diamond tip. Or perhaps the stabbing quality of the steel.

Both Stratton men were stunned. Was she actually repositioning her hat? Or was she making, so to speak, a veiled threat?

"Young ladies," said Mr. Stratton senior, refusing to focus on the gleaming hat pin, "do not talk back to their fathers."

Strat forced himself to put Miss Lockwood out of his thoughts. He had to end this scene, whatever it was. Folding his arms over his chest, trying to take up more space against the great space his father's chest consumed, he said, "Father, perhaps you and I should be the ones to go to the village and discuss Florinda's evidence with the police."

"Florinda's *evidence*? You have never cared a whit for Florinda's word or opinion until now. And you've been correct. Florinda rarely gets anything right. She didn't get this right either."

"Why are you so eager to have Bridget be responsible?" cried Devonny.

"Because nobody else could be! Do you think one of *us* pushed Matthew?"

Devonny believed Florinda. Which meant Mr. Rowwells had lied, and since Devonny also believed Bridget, so had Walk lied. Why lie? Did they have two different reasons, or one shared reason? "If Florinda is right—"

"Devonny," said her father, pulling his lips back from his teeth like a rabid dog, "go to your room. Florinda, wait for me in my library. The topic of servants is closed."

I'll go into town to collect Bridget, thought Strat. Then what will I do with her? I can't have her around Devonny. Think how Bridget behaved with Walk! I'll have to give her money, I guess, to make up for this, and put her on a train, or—

But Florinda had not moved. "Hiram, I will not have Bridget punished for something she did not do."

The sunny day seemed to condense and darken around them. For a moment Strat thought it was time falling; that Annie would come back in such a darkness; but it was his father's fury that darkened the world.

"And I will not have a wife who disobeys," said Hiram Stratton, Sr. "You may do as you were told, Florinda, or you may prepare yourself not to be my wife."

"What do you mean, where was I? None of your business, Sean!" shouted Annie. Any ladylike behavior she might have picked up in 1895 was quickly discarded. Ladylike meant people ran over you. Forget that. Annie was in the mood to run over others, not to be run over herself.

She would have guessed Sean's reaction and she would have been wrong. Big, tough, old Sean wilted. "I'm sorry, Annie," he said humbly. "I was so worried. You just disappeared. One minute you were there and the next minute you weren't. There was no trace of you." Sean looked at her nervously. "Who were you with?"

Why was everybody so sure she'd been with somebody? If a person chose to vanish, she could do it all by herself. "I fell asleep on the sand," she said sharply. This was beginning to sound quite possible, even reasonable. Annie could almost picture the cozy little sun-drenched beach where it had happened.

"Come on, ASL. Since Friday afternoon? When half the town was looking for you?"

"Half the town did not look for me," she said, trying to distract him.

"The half that knows you went looking," he said. "Your friends. Your family. Your neighbors. The cops. People on the beach who were sick of getting tans. We were afraid you'd fallen through a floor in the Mansion or gone swimming in a riptide. You scared people." Sean kicked the carpet with his huge dirty sneaker toe. "You owe me an explanation."

I am a century changer, she thought. I have visited both sides of time. People think they own time. They have watches and clocks and digital pulses. But they are wrong. *Time owns them.* I am the property of Time, just as Harriett will be the property of her husband.

"Your face changed," said Sean. "Tell me, Annie. Tell me who you were with and what you were doing."

I was with Strat. What if I never see him again, never touch him, never kiss, never have a photograph?

She was swept up by physical remembrance: the set of his chin, the sparkle in his eyes, the antiqueness of his haircut. Oh Strat! her heart cried.

How dare Sean exist when Strat did not? But then, how was Sean supposed to know that he didn't measure up to somebody a hundred years ago?

I failed Time, which brought me through. I didn't do my assignment. How easily Time can punish me! All it has to do is not give me Strat again. What if I pull it off, and change centuries once more, and Time punishes me by sending me to Tutankhamen? Or Marie Antoinette? Or even an empty Stratton Beach before settlement: just me and the seagulls and the piles of oyster shells?

"I'll forgive you," said Sean. "I can get past it."

"Pond scum!" shouted Annie. She looked around for something to throw at him. "Forgive me for what? Get past what? You do not own me, Sean, and wherever I was is none of your business. So there. I'm breaking up with you anyway. It's over. Go home."

I am a mean, bad, rotten person, she thought. How could Sean have any idea what I'm talking about? I'm doing this too roughly, too fast. But I have places to go!

I have to get back, I cannot give Strat up. A minute

148

ago I thought I had to, but I don't. I can have it all, I'm sure of that. Somehow I can go back, but not upset Mom and Dad. Somehow with or without me around, they'll keep the marriage alive so that when I do get back . . .

I cannot have it all.

If Mom can't have it all—career, family, husband, success, happiness, fidelity—how could I possibly think I could have it all? In two separate centuries yet? I can have one or the other, but I cannot have both.

Sean was trying to argue, but she had lost interest in Sean, exactly as Strat had lost interest in Harriett.

Oh, Harriett! You were kind to me, and loaned me your gowns, and did what you knew Strat wanted you to do, and where did you end up? Alone. Abandoned. And hurt so badly that you accepted a marriage proposal from a man nobody could like.

Life interfered yet again. Heather and Kelly stormed in. They were just as mad at Annie as everybody else. Maybe it was true that half the town had been searching for her.

Heather and Kelly didn't believe a single syllable of the sleeping-on-the-sand nonsense. "You better tell us what really happened," said Heather, "or our friendship is sleeping on the sand, too."

"I was time traveling," said Annie, to see how they reacted. "I fell back a hundred years to find out what the Mansion was really like." A huge lump filled her throat. She could at least have left Harriett and Strat to live happily ever after. But no, Bridget would be hung and Harriett would marry that Rowwells creep.

And if I *could* go back, she thought, I'm so selfish that I'd keep Strat. Harriett would still have to marry her creep.

"Annie, this is when people hire firing squads to do away with a person," explained Kelly. "People who say they were time traveling get executed by their best friends. Sean, get lost. She'll tell us if you're not here."

They were right. Annie would tell everything. Girls did.

The problem, however, thought Annie, is that I can tell you everything, but you cannot possibly believe everything.

"I'll wait in my car," said Sean. "I'll wait fifteen minutes, and then ASL and I are going for a drive."

"Don't make it sound so threatening," said Annie.

"I'll take you to Mickey D's," said Sean. "I'll buy you a hamburger."

Annie was not thrilled. Sean's offer did not compare to the offers made in other centuries.

"And fries," Sean said. "And a vanilla milkshake."

Annie remained unthrilled.

"Okay, okay. You can have a Big Mac."

Romance in my century, she thought, is pitiful. "Fine. Sit in the car," said Annie.

The instant the door shut behind Sean, Kelly said, "I demand to know the boy you were with, and exactly, anatomically, what you were doing all night long."

How shocked Harriett and Devonny would have been. The idea that a lady might have "done" something would be unthinkable. Strat, too, would be appalled. Ladies weren't even supposed to know what "something" was, let alone do it. They'd *really* be shocked if Kelly hadn't used careful polite phrasing just in case Annie's parents were around to overhear.

I did something, thought Annie, starting to cry. I hurt people on both sides of time.

Devonny went into the library with Florinda.

I hate men, she thought. I hate marriage. I hate what happened to Mother and to Florinda and next to Harriett and soon to me. Men ruling.

Suddenly her silly stepmother seemed very precious, the one that Devonny had always wanted to keep. Mean and harsh as Father was, to be without him would be starvation and social suicide for Florinda. "Florinda, was Bridget really with you?"

"Of course she was really with me. Why would I lie?"

"If you aren't lying, Mr. Rowwells is."

"Gentlemen never lie," said Florinda, with a desperate sarcasm.

"Father lies to you all the time and you spend half your life having vapors because of it."

"You mustn't speak that way of your father," said Florinda, with no spirit. No hope.

"Florinda, we must get Bridget out of jail."

"I have been told not to bring up the subject again."

"You must call the police and tell them that Bridget was with you and they will release her."

"I can't use the telephone without permission," said Florinda.

"I did."

"You're a child, you can get away with things. Your father adores you, but he doesn't adore me, I haven't given him a son, in fact his last two wives haven't given him sons either, and he's tired of me and I cannot argue anymore. Devonny, I have nowhere else to go."

Father had to provide for Mama because Strat and I would not have tolerated anything else, thought Devonny. But he doesn't have to provide for Florinda because she produced no children.

Florinda's small elegant hand tucked around Devonny's. They were both crying. "Bridget turned Walk down, Devonny, anybody could see that. Bridget's mistake was not letting him have his way. That's the rule, Devonny. They must have their way."

Why can't we ever have our way? thought Devonny Stratton. Why must Harriett be Mr. Rowwells' property? Why must I be Father's?

She looked at her stepmother, frail and lovely, like a torn butterfly wing, and thought how Father would love an oil portrait of Florinda as she was now: pale and submissive and trembling.

CHAPTER 11

The second week after school ended, fewer teenagers congregated at the beach. Many had started their summer jobs. They were selling ice cream and hamburgers, mowing lawns and repairing gutters, sweating in assembly lines and teaching swimming. They were visiting cousins and going to Disney World and babysitting for neighbors.

Annie's job was at Ice Kreem King, a beach concession that sold soft ice cream treats, candy bars and saltwater taffy. It was sticky work. Nobody wanted a plain vanilla cone. They wanted a sundae with strawberries and walnuts and whipped cream, or a double-decker peanut butter parfait. Annie wore white Bermuda shorts, a white shirt with a little green Ice Kreem King logo and a white baseball cap, backwards. Over this she wore a huge white apron now sloshed with dip: lime, strawberry, cherry, chocolate and banana frosted her front.

It was hard to believe in the lives of Florinda, Devonny and Harriett at a time like this.

It was all too possible to believe in her own life.

Her desperate mother was even more torn between reality and dream than Annie. Mom loved work, even loved her commute to New York, because she read her precious newspapers on the train: *The Wall Street Journal* and *The New York Times*. Mom didn't even buy them now. Her hands shook when she tried to fold the paper the way train readers do to avoid hitting fellow passengers. Her eyes blurred when she tried to read the tiny print of the financial pages. She couldn't concentrate.

It was easy to know what Mom wanted. She wanted her marriage back. She wanted her happiness and safety back.

It was even easier to know what Dad wanted: he wanted it all.

Miss Bartten had gotten very bold, and even phoned him at home.

Tod, who loved the telephone, and maintained friendships across the country with people he didn't care about so he could call long distance at night, would no longer answer the phone. The answering machine was like a crude, loudmouthed servant. Miss Bartten's bright voice kept getting preserved there, demanding Dad call her back.

And he did.

Nobody was taking steps to resolve anything.

They seemed to be hoping Time would do that for them.

For Annie Lockwood, Time achieved a power and dimension that made clocks and calendars silly.

By day, Annie was a servant to the ice cream whims of a vast beachgoing public. Each evening, she and whatever family members were there for dinner ate separately, trying not to touch bodies or thoughts or pain. Annie had no idea how to help her mother and no interest in helping her father. And yet she, too, wanted their marriage back and their love back.

Since she'd broken up with Sean, girls kept asking who would replace him.

In her heart, Annie had Strat, who was no replacement for anybody; he was first and only. Beneath her pillow lay a neatly folded white gown with hand-sewn pleats. She wept into it, soaking it with pointless tears, as if those century-old stitches could telegraph to Strat that she was still here, still in love with him.

She felt at night like a plane flying in the misty clouds: no horizon, no landmarks, no nothing. Oh, Strat, if I had you I would be all right. And what about you? Are you all right? Are there landmarks and horizons for you? Do you remember me?

Devonny was boosted up into the carriage by servants, while Florinda helped lift the skirt of Devonny's traveling gown. Strat and Devonny were being shipped back to New York City. Walk was to go along, so Strat would have normal masculine company and not mope around stroking doorknobs and mirrors as if Miss Lockwood might suddenly pop out.

The first time Father overheard Strat actually calling out loud to a girl he then explained had been missing a hundred years, Father thrashed him. Took his riding boots off and whaled Strat with them. Strat hardly noticed, but returned to the Great Hall, where, he claimed, he had witnessed Anna Sophia's birth. This time Father chose a whip, the one Robert, the coachman, used on the horses, Strat noticed. He didn't call Anna Sophia again. But he looked for her. His eyes would travel strangely, as if trying to peer beyond things, or through them, or into their history.

Father was fearful that Strat was losing his sanity and had even communicated with Mother on the subject. The final decision was in favor of a change of air. Fresh air was an excellent solution to so many health problems.

Most houseguests were long gone, but Harriett would of course remain at the Mansion while Father and Mr. Rowwells continued to work on the marriage arrangements.

Florinda had refused to let go of the topic of Bridget and the parasol. Finally Father had gone down to the police, and Bridget had been set free. How Devonny wanted to see Bridget again! She yearned to apologize for what Bridget had endured, see if Jeb had visited and give Bridget some of her old dresses to make up for it, but of course Father would not have Bridget brought back into the household after her loose behavior with Walk.

Florinda could not persuade Father that Walk might have lied, or been the one who was in the wrong. When girls like Bridget did not cooperate, they must be dismissed. But she had won Bridget's freedom, and that success gave Florinda pride.

Summertime had failed Devonny. It was not the slow warm yellow time she looked forward to. Not the salty soft airy time it had been every other summer. It was full of fear and anger and worry.

Now they were losing their usual months at the beach, losing the Mansion and tennis and golf and sand. They were losing Harriett; and Strat of course had lost Miss Lockwood. Devonny's lips rested on Florinda's cool paper-white skin, skin never ever exposed to sun, and whispered, "Will you be all right?"

They both knew that if Father got rid of her, she would never be all right, and if Father kept her, he might be so rough and mean that she would never be all right either.

Visions of her father's rage kept returning to Devonny. Who else but Father himself could get angry enough to push—

No. Even inside her head, in the deepest, most distant corners of her mind, Devonny could not have such a traitorous thought.

"I will be fine," said Florinda, kissing her back. "Say hello to your dear mother for me, and visit the Statue of Liberty, and send me postcards."

Postcards were the rage. Florinda sent dozens every week. They had had their own postcards made up for the Mansion, its views and ornate buildings. "I'll write," promised Devonny.

Trunks, hatboxes and valises were strapped on top and stacked inside the carriage. It was four miles to the railroad station, where their private railroad car would be waiting for them. Devonny knew where Jeb's family lived. She was hoping that when the carriage went by, she'd see Bridget, leaning on Jeb's strong arm, or sweeping Jeb's porch, and she would know that Bridget was all right.

"Here, sit by me," said Walker Walkley, smiling wonderfully.

It certainly went to show that you could not judge a person by his smile. Devonny said, "Thank you, Walk, but I like to ride facing forward. I'll sit next to Strat." She kissed Florinda one last time, wondering if it really was the last time.

Walk made Strat change sides of the carriage so that he was sitting next to Devonny after all.

Heather and Kelly, part of the not-working group, picked their way past a thousand beach blankets and towels, looking for their own crowd's space on the sand. Nobody actually went into the ocean and got wet. If you wanted to swim, you went to somebody's house with a pool. The beach was for tans and company and most of all for showing off one's physique.

Sean had a spectacular physique. He was showing off most of it. There was not a girl on the beach who could figure out why Annie Lockwood had dumped him. Was she insane?

"Annie's afternoon break is at three," said Kelly. "I'll go get her and she can hang out with us for fifteen minutes."

Sean shrugged as if he didn't care, and then said, "I always thought we'd get married or something." He kicked sand.

"*Married?*" Heather laughed. "Sean, you two never even went to the movies together!"

"I know, but I sort of figured that's how it would go. ASL can't break up with me." Sean shoveled the sand with his big feet. In moments he had a major ditch.

"What's the trench for?" asked a boy named Cody. "You starting a war here, Sean?"

"He's trying to make peace," said Kelly, hoping Cody would notice her. Kelly had always wanted to go out with Cody.

"Annie Lockwood is only a girl, Sean," Cody said. "She's nothing. Forget her. The beach is full of girls. Just pick one. They're all alike and who cares?"

Cody was not her dream man after all. Kelly crossed the hot sand to get Annie from the concession booth. She wasn't friends with Annie this summer the way she'd expected to be. Annie felt like two different people. As if she'd left some of herself someplace. It was creepy.

*   *   *

159

"Do you think Harriett will be all right?" said Devonny.

"She'll be fine," said Strat.

"Do you think Father will still let her go to college?"

"I would hope not," said Walk. "Live by herself in some wicked godless institution? The sooner they wed, the better."

"You're going to college," Devonny pointed out.

"We're men. Young ladies are ruined by such things."

Young ladies are ruined by things like you, thought Devonny. She flounced on the seat and moved the draperies away from the window, staring out at the empty dunes and the shrieking terns.

Strat was overcome with guilt about Harriett. His good friend, and he had abandoned her to a winter marriage. A marriage with no summer in it. No laughter, no warmth, no dancing, no joy. Just money and suitability.

He had caused this and he knew it, but every time he tried to wish it undone, he thought of Miss Lockwood. It was more than thinking of her: it was drowning in her.

The carriage moved slowly around the curving lanes, through the golf course, past the ledge where you could see distant islands, and down again where you could see only the lily pond and the back of the Mansion.

Cherry Lane, he thought. Annie's house was built in the cherry orchard. If I went there, and called her name . . . I could tell Robert to halt the carriage by the cherry orchard. I could run through the grass and the trees calling her name, and maybe . . .

Walk would report to Father, Father would decide Strat had gone insane, and would choose an asylum on a lake where Strat would be strapped to an iron bed and given cold water and brown bread.

He tried to school Annie out of his mind. Tried to carve her memory out of his heart.

But he too moved the draperies aside to stare out the window.

"What do you want to break up for?" said Sean.

That Sean would be shattered was the last thing Annie had expected. She hadn't thought Sean even liked her very much. She certainly hadn't thought his eyes could produce tears. Every time the two of them talked, he'd rub the back of his hand hard against his eyes, which grew redder and wetter. Annie felt nothing.

"You don't even care, do you?" whispered Sean.

Why didn't people take things the way you planned for them to? She wanted to be nice to Sean. She wanted to break up easily. He wasn't cooperating. "I'm sorry, Sean, but we never did much of anything, and the only time you ever spoke to me was to ask me to get you a wrench or something. You never said—" She didn't want to use the word love; the timing was impossible; if she said love, it would give a second-rate high school relationship something it had never had. "You never said you cared much, Sean."

She was afraid she might actually try to define love for Sean: she might actually tell him about Strat.

Sean was dragging out a cotton handkerchief now and mopping up his face. The beach crowd thinned out. People like Cody decided that even swimming was better than seeing a boy crack up in public over a girl. "ASL, we have the whole summer in front of us," said Sean. "I want to spend the summer together."

Doing what? Rebuilding the transmission on your car? "Sean, I'm really, really sorry, but I think it's time for us to break up."

"It isn't time! I love you!"

Wonderful. Now he had to love her. Now when she—

When I what? thought Annie. When I have Strat? I don't have Strat. I don't even know where Strat is, or if he ever was.

She rallied. "And stop calling me ASL. It's dumb and I'm through with it."

"The way you're through with me? You're going to throw me out like a lousy nickname?" Sean muttered on and on, like a toddler who was sure that if he just whined long enough his mother would break down and buy him the sugar cereal with the purple prize.

Summer time is actually a different sort of time, thought Annie. It lasts longer and has more repeats, more sun, and more heat. We'll have these same conversations day after day, stuck in time. Now, when I want to travel in time.

Time did not stand still. Somehow you could go back and possess time gone by, but your own natural time continued.

Summer when her parents would decide what to do with their failing marriage. Summer when their daughter would vanish forever, without a trace? How could she do that to them? It would be pure self-indulgence to dip back into the past century. Dad was self-indulgent. He should have stopped himself.

Annie must stop herself. These were real lives, all around her, both sides of time. Real people were really hurt. If she went back, it would be pure self-indulgence. Exactly the same as Dad going back to Miss Bartten.

I can't go back just because I was pampered and coddled and dressed so beautifully. I can't go back just to find out what happens to them. I can't go back just to see if Florinda is still arranging flowers and Genevieve is still asking for a donation and Devonny gets to go to college and Gertrude volunteers for the Red Cross.

I must stop myself and not go back. Look what I did to Harriett's life by entering it. And Bridget. It's been ten days for me, so it's been ten for Bridget.

Clearer than any of them, clearer even than Strat, she saw Aunt Ada: toothless mouth and envelope lips, eyes glittering with secrets. She could actually feel, like velvet or silk, the emotions that had roiled through that elegant ballroom, jealousy and greed filtering through the lace of hope and love.

"Oh, Annie! Pay attention for once! You're so annoying," said Heather. She pointed down the beach, where Sean had joined Cody in the water. "He's better than nothing! What are you going to replace him with?"

"Sean isn't a mug. He didn't fall off the shelf and break, so I don't need to replace him."

But could I go back for love? I love Strat. Strat loves me. Is that a good enough reason to hurt two families? It's good enough for Miss Bartten.

Heather, who didn't have a boyfriend, was very into other girls' boyfriends. "Summertime, and you throw away a handsome popular interesting guy?"

Annie pointed out an unfortunate fact. "Sean is only handsome and popular. He isn't interesting."

"So who were you with all night at the beach?" said Kelly softly, coaxingly.

A odd distant boom sounded. Kettle drums, maybe? The beginning of a symphony? But also like a car crash, miles away.

Hundreds of beachgoers turned, bodies tilted to listen. Cody and Sean and the rest took a single step back to dry sand.

The boom repeated: this time with vibration, as if some giant possessed a boom box loud enough to fibrillate hearts. They felt the boom through the bottoms of their bare feet.

"The Mansion!" yelled Sean, first to figure it out. "They're ahead of schedule! They've started knocking it down." Girls moved to the back of his priorities, the way girls should. "Come on," he yelled. "Let's go watch the demolition."

*   *   *

Annie Lockwood screamed his name once, the single syllable streaking through the air like the cry of a white tern protecting its nest. *"Strat!"* And then she was running. She fought the sand, which sucked up her flimsy little sneakers, and she made it to the pavement, and ran faster than she had ever run anyplace. Against her white shorts and shirt, her bare legs and arms looked truly gold.

If the Mansion came down . . . if there was nothing left . . . *how would she ever get back?*

"Strat!"

The wrecking ball, a ton of swinging iron, was indifferent to the shrieks of a teenage girl on a distant path. Massive chains attached it to a great crane. It hit the far turret, from which Harriett had once looked out across the sand and watched Strat fall in love. The tower splintered in half but did not fall, and the wrecking ball swung backward, preparing for its next pass.

Annie felt as if it hit her own stomach. *How will I get back if there is nothing left but splinters?*

Blinking lights and sawhorses stood in her path. Signs proclaimed danger. "You can't go no further today," said a burly man in a yellow hard hat. He was chewing tobacco and spitting. "It's dangerous. No souvenirs."

I don't want a souvenir. I want Strat.

She had never wanted anything so much in her life, or dreamed of wanting anything so much. She could have turned herself inside out, peeled herself

165

away from the year, thrown herself like a ton of swinging iron a hundred years away.

"Strat!" she screamed.

Strat ripped open the carriage door and leaped out while the four horses were still clippy-clopping along. Robert, the driver, yanked them to a stop. Strat was yelling incoherently, dancing like a maniac in the middle of the road.

Walker Walkley was pleased. If Strat were to go insane, he, Walk, could not only marry Devonny, but he could become the replacement son. They were barely a few hundred yards from the Mansion. Robert was a solid witness and would testify to young Mr. Stratton's seizure. This was good.

Devonny was frantic. If Strat were to go insane, she, Devonny, would have to protect him. And how was she going to do that, when she had failed to protect either Bridget or Florinda?

Through the open swinging carriage door, Walker Walkley saw it happen. Anna Sophia Lockwood. Transparent. And then translucent. And then solid.

His hair crawled. His spine turned to ice and his tongue tasted like rust. *There are ghosts.*

"Annie!" said Strat, laughing and laughing and laughing. He swung her in a circle, while he kissed her flying hair. "Robert!" he yelled, remembering the trouble he was in. He almost threw Annie into the carriage with Devonny and Walk. "Hurry on, Robert, forget this, you didn't see a thing."

Robert, probably knowing what a large tip he would get, obeyed.

Devonny shrieked, "Strat! She's naked. And she may be a murderer. Don't you put her in here with me. Where did she come from? Where are her clothes?"

"She isn't a murderer, Dev. I don't know who did it, but it wasn't Annie, she wasn't here yet, I saw her coming the last time and I know."

"Saw her coming?" repeated Devonny.

Walk, who had just seen what Strat meant, scrunched into his corner, unwilling to be touched by the flesh of a ghost.

"She did travel over the century?" whispered Devonny.

"Of course," said her brother.

They're all insane, thought Walker. Do I really want to marry Devonny and have that insanity pass to my children?

"Well!" said Devonny, gathering herself together. "She can't sit here with nothing on. Walk, close your eyes. Strat, turn your back. Thank goodness I have a valise in here." Devonny undid the straps of a huge leather satchel and pulled out a gown to cover the girl up.

Walk put his hands over his eyes, but naturally stared through his fingers anyway. Every inch of her was beautiful. All that skin! Husbands didn't see that much of their wives. Nevertheless, Walker did not envy Strat. Nothing would have made him touch a female who came and went by ghost.

Sean of course had taken his car.

He wouldn't waste time floundering over sand and grass when he could drive. He saw his girlfriend running and tried to clock her, because she was really moving. She should take up track. When ASL twisted through the woods, he could see her no longer. But he knew the name now. The guy she'd spent the night on the beach with. Scott or Skip or something. Whoever it was, Sean would beat him up. No Skippie or Scottie was fooling around with Sean's girl.

Sean felt great.

He'd show Skippie a thing or two.

His car came around the long curve from which the Mansion was most visible. He saw the wrecking ball hit the square turret and stopped his car in awe. There was nothing like destruction.

And he saw Annie Lockwood.

Her dark hair, half braided, and now half loose, was oddly cloudy. He meant to drive toward her, but he had the odd, and then terrifying, sense that the road was full. He could see nothing on the road. Only he, Sean, occupied that road, *and yet it was full.*

He half dreaded a collision, and yet there was nothing there with which to collide.

He half waited, and half saw Annie slip through time, and had half a story to tell when people demanded answers.

CHAPTER 12

It had been hard to believe when it happened before—centuries grazing her cheeks and swirling through her hair. But this time—as if a godmother waved a wand—time simply shifted. There was no falling, no rush of years roaring in her ears.

I didn't touch anything magic, thought Annie. There was nothing to touch. So what does it? Is it true love? Did he call me back, or did I call him back?

She was wild with joy, and did not want to let go of him. His lovely neck, his perfect hair, his great shoulders—but here was Devonny demanding to know why she was naked. "I'm not naked. I'm wearing plenty of clothes," she protested. "Shorts and shirt, clean and white."

"You are disgusting," said Devonny. "But I suppose murderers are." She pulled out an Empire-style dress of pale blue, embroidered with darker blue flowers and white leaves, a dress so decorative Annie felt she had turned into a painting to go over a mantel. It was very tight by Annie's standards, but these people wanted their clothes to be like capsules.

"I'm not a murderer, Devonny," said Annie. I'm so happy to see her! thought Annie. Has it been a hundred years or ten days since we talked last?

Devonny gave the boys permission to look again.

Strat and Annie looked at each other with smiles so wide they couldn't kiss, couldn't pull their lips together long enough to manage kisses. For once Devonny actually met Walk's eyes, and together they squinted with a complete lack of appreciation. Strat should not be in love with a possible murderess, lunatic or century changer.

"Strat and Devonny and I are quite frantic to see the Statue of Liberty, Miss Lockwood," said Walker Walkley, to interrupt this unseemly display, "and are going into the city for a change of air."

Devonny produced a large oval cardboard box, papered, ribboned and tied like a birthday present. From this she drew out a truly hideous straw contraption, with tilted double brims, decorated with wrens in nests that dripped with yellow berries.

"I have not been frantic to see the Statue of Liberty," Strat corrected. "I have been frantic to see Anna Sophia."

Roughly Devonny pinned up Annie's hair, stabbing her head several times, just the way Annie would have if she'd been as irritated with *her* brother's choice of girlfriend. Slanting the grotesque hat on Annie's head,

Devonny flourished a pin with a glittering evil point. Annie flinched.

"Don't worry. People hardly ever get killed with hat pins," said Strat, grinning. "It is essential to be in fashion."

"No wonder your courtship has to be so formal," said Annie. "We can't both get under the brim of the hat to kiss. I refuse to wear this." She was sure Strat would hurl the hideous thing out the carriage window, but instead he tied it beneath her chin and secured the veiling that hid her neck, throat and cheeks.

"No way!" cried Annie. Trying to see through the veil was like holding a thin envelope up to the sun to try to read the contents.

But Strat would not let her take the hat and veiling off. "I'm thinking as fast as I can," said Strat, his mood swerving from love to responsibility. "Father is in a terrible mood. Finding you will make things worse, so we won't let him know. You'll come into the city with us, that's how I'll protect you. You'll be a friend of Devonny's. We'll smuggle you into the railroad car, and—"

"She won't be a friend of mine," said Devonny. "She killed Matthew."

"Devonny, will you be quiet?" said her brother. "She did not kill Matthew."

"Then who did?" demanded Devonny. "Bridget was in the garden with Florinda when Matthew was pushed down the stairs. Mr. Rowwells saw some young girl do it, and it wasn't Bridget, so it had to be her."

Behind veils and ribbons and straw and birds' nests, Annie tried to think. But they planned their fashion well, these people who did not want women to think. The heavy gloves, the tightly buttoned dress bodice, the pins and ties and bows—they removed Annie from Strat, removed her from clear thought, made of her a true store-window mannequin. Merely an upright creature on which to hang clothing.

"They'll hang you," said Devonny to Annie, "but at least you'll have clothes on."

"They'll hang me?" For a moment Annie had no working parts. No lungs, no heart, no brain.

Strat flung himself around her. "I won't let them touch you. They have no proof, and I saw you come through, so I know you didn't do it. I will save you, Annie."

"Strat, this isn't a good idea," said Walker Walkley. "Your sister has undoubtedly guessed correctly. Your father forgave you for what happened with Harriett, but he won't forgive you for sheltering a murderess. Put this female out on the road and let the police find her."

The police? thought Annie. If they were that mad at me for wasting their time on a search, how mad will they be if they think I murdered somebody? Would they really hang me? What would I say at my trial? *No, at the time I was a hundred years later.* Not a great defense. *I sort of saw what happened, it was very dark, and the blackness rasped around me, and . . .* Oh, the jury would love it. All the way to the gallows.

Her mouth was terribly dry. She had no corset this

time, but even so, she could not get enough breath. She had thought only of love, not of consequence.

"We need to go into New York on schedule, Strat," said Walk, "and not refer to this again. Your father will lock you up too. You must think clearly. There is a lot at stake here."

"Annie's life and freedom are at stake," said Strat intensely. He moved her forward on the seat, putting his own arm and chest behind her, so he was protecting her back, even in the carriage.

He meant it. Her life and freedom. At stake.

Stake. Did they use stakes in 1895? Did they tie women to poles and burn them? Surely that was two centuries earlier.

Nothing felt real. Not her body, not her hands inside the heavy gloves, not Strat on the other side of the veil.

"Would they really hang me?" whispered Annie.

"I won't let them," said Strat.

Which meant they would . . . if they caught her.

Harriett was wearing a similar hat. By tying the veil completely over her face, claiming fear of sun, she could prevent Mr. Rowwells from touching her skin. It was very hot, yet not a single inch of Harriett's skin was exposed. She wore long sleeves, hat, veil, gloves and buttoned boots.

How could Devonny and Strat leave me here like this!

Tears slid down her face behind the veil.

But by accepting a marriage proposal, she had become a different person; property instead of a young girl. Until the agreements were settled, she could not be taking excursions. She must stay here with her guardian and her fiancé.

When Harriett had asked about college, Mr. Stratton simply looked at her. "You made a decision, Harriett, of which you knew I would disapprove. College is not a possibility."

She wanted to throw herself on his mercy, and say she was sorry, and she was afraid of Mr. Rowwells, and she loved Strat, and she would give all her money to the Strattons forever if she could just cancel this engagement, but something in Mr. Stratton's eyes filled Harriett with anger: that this should be her lot in life, to obey.

So she let it go on, when the only way it could go was worse.

"I wanted to do the right thing by you," said Jeb through the bars. "So I came to say good-bye."

"And how is that the right thing?" said Bridget, her temper flaring. She did not come close to him. She was too filthy now, and could not bear for Jeb to see her like this, especially when he was not coming from love, but duty.

"I was wrong to step out with you," said Jeb. She thought perhaps his cheeks colored, saying that, but there was so little light from the lantern the jailer held that she couldn't be sure. "My father and mother are giving me the money to head West. I'm going to try California. I have my train ticket." Jeb forgot he was a man leaving a woman, and said excitedly, "You can go all the way by train now. I'll see buffalo and Indians, Bridget. I'll see prairies and the Rocky Mountains and the Pacific Ocean."

"Yes, and I hope you'll see the devil too," snapped Bridget. She was crying. She wanted to stay strong, but he was leaving her and she did not have a friend in the world who could get her out of this. The other servants had crept by, one by one, bringing better food and trying to bring courage, but they could not bring hope.

After all, Bridget came close to the boy she had loved, overcome by terror and loneliness. "Jeb, please! Go to the Mansion and—"

"Bridget, I'm taking the next train. You attacked Matthew, and there was no reason but your Irish temper, and you have to pay now."

And he was gone.

And with him the jailer, and the lantern, and the last light she ever expected to see before her trial.

Florinda and Harriett circled the garden. Florinda was wearing less protection from the sun than Harriett, but they were both gasping for breath. "I have just learned something dreadful," said Florinda.

Everything was dreadful now, so Harriett did not bother to respond.

"He lied," said Florinda. "Hiram told us he went to the police and explained about Bridget, but Hiram didn't go at all. Bridget is still in jail and nobody in authority knows that she was with me when Matthew was murdered."

Harriett stared at Florinda. "He lied? But why, Florinda? Why would he lie to us?"

"I expect because it's easier. Bridget is just a servant and we are just women."

"I don't want to be *just* a woman!"

"You have money of your own," Florinda pointed out. "You could choose not to marry and never have that cigar-smoking lump touch you."

Harriett did not argue with this insulting description. "I gave my word."

"Yes, well, they break their word all the time, don't they?"

The gentlemen appeared on the veranda.

How frightening they were, in those buttoned waistcoats and high collars, with those black lines running down the fabric, as if attaching them to the earth they owned. Like judges at the end of the world, thought Harriett. If only I could be permitted to judge them instead!

Mr. Stratton actually snapped his fingers to call Florinda. He was having a brandy, and wished her company. Briefly. He just liked to look at her, and then would dismiss her. She was a property, a nice one, but on trial herself now, and might soon be replaced.

Florinda bowed her head and obeyed.

Harriett was getting a terrible headache. Far too much heat trapped in far too much clothing. Far too many terrible thoughts in far too short a time.

For who had the worst temper of anyone on the estate?

Mr. Stratton.

Who struck people who could not strike back?

Mr. Stratton.

Who had lied about rescuing Bridget, and was allowing a young girl to carry the blame for a murder?

Mr. Stratton.

Harriett followed Florinda slowly. Nobody would question her laggard pace. Ladies were expected to be leisurely. Once she went indoors, she would have to remove the hat and veil. It would take all her control to keep a calm face. She could not imagine ever looking at the face of Mr. Stratton again. Like Florinda, she would have to keep her head bowed and her eyes averted. There was no point in begging Mr. Stratton again to help Bridget.

In this heat, in this shock of knowledge, Harriett could see little point in anything.

"Sherry," Mr. Rowwells told the servant. "And what will you have, my dear?"

"Lemonade, please," said Harriett.

Aunt Ada did not join them. Mr. Stratton was as angry at Ada as he was at Strat over this fiasco. Yet Ada did not seem to mind, or to be afraid, in the way that Florinda minded and was afraid.

Ada was far more at risk than even Florinda, though. Ada had nothing, absolutely nothing, not a stick of furniture nor a penny in savings. Yet Ada was calm. Spinsters dependent on unpleasant relatives did not normally experience calm. What did that mean? Was Ada no longer dependent?

"Well, Rowwells," said Mr. Stratton. "Golf this afternoon?"

"I think I need to spend time with my fiancée instead," said Mr. Rowwells. He smiled at Harriet, who managed not to shudder.

He wants to be kind, she said to herself. He wants me to love him. He wants my money, but after all, we must get along as well. I must make an effort. The quicker I allow Mr. Rowwells to accomplish this marriage, the quicker I will get out of the house of a man who shoves servants down stairs instead of just firing them. How could a gentleman care enough about a servant to bother with killing one? What could Matthew have done or said to make Mr. Stratton so angry?

"What might you and I do this afternoon, Harriett?" said the man with whom she would spend her life.

I shall pretend to be Anna Sophia, thought Harriett. I shall pretend to be a beautiful creature with lovely hair and trembling mouth. I shall pretend that it is Strat who loves me, and Strat who holds my hand. I wonder if I can keep up such a pretense for an entire marriage. Perhaps I will die in childbirth and be saved from a long marriage.

"Mr. Rowwells," she said, "on such a day I would love to sit in the tower, and feel the ocean breeze. With you at my side."

Mr. Rowwells was delighted. At last this difficult fiancée was showing some proper affection.

Up the massive central stairs they went, Harriett first. Down the guest wing and up the narrower steps to the next floor. And then up the curving beauty of the tower stairs, like a Renaissance lighthouse, painted with a sky of cherubs, clouds and flowers.

The tower was furnished, of course, because the Mansion had no empty corners, jammed with seats and pillows and knickknacks and objects. A tiny desk on which to take notes about migrating birds or lunar eclipses balanced precariously. No one, in fact, had ever taken notes on anything.

But paper lay on the desk, ink filled the little glass well and a pen lay waiting on the polished surface.

It seemed to Harriett that her entire life lay waiting on a polished surface.

She looked out across the white empty sand where only a few days ago her life had fallen apart, when the boy she loved found another to love.

A private railroad car!

Annie had learned about these in American history, but she didn't know they were still around. Then she remembered that they weren't *still* around; she was back when they *were* around.

It was beyond twentieth-century belief.

Oriental carpet covered floors, walls, window brackets and ceiling. Every shade and flavor of cinnamon and wine and ruby filled the room. Fatly stuffed sofas and chairs were hung with swirling gold fringe.

Brass lights with glittering glass cups arched from the walls.

Wearing a veil indoors was rather like wearing very dark sunglasses. She adjusted the veil, feeling like an Arab woman peering out the slits of her robe.

"Hello, Stephens," said Devonny to a uniformed waiter. Or servant. Or railroad officer. He too dripped gold. "This is Miss Ethel St. John, who will be traveling with us. Miss St. John does not feel well and will use Miss Florinda's stateroom."

Ethel! thought Annie. Where do they dredge up these names? Hiram, Harriett, Clarence, Gertrude and now Ethel! At least it makes Anna Sophia sound pretty.

Strat led her to a bulging crimson sofa strewn with furniture scarves, and sat her down. He unfastened the ribbons that tied her hat beneath her chin and tucked back the veil like a groom finding his bride. "I love you, Annie," he whispered.

Her heart turned over. How physically, how completely, love came, like drowning or falling. He would take care of her, and how wonderful it would be. No cares.

We will go into Manhattan, and I will find out what a town house is, and see New York City a hundred years ago. I will become clever at the piano, and spend time on my correspondence. Devonny and Florinda and I will dress in fashions as beautiful as brides all day long. No more striving to be best, or even just to live through all those tests of school and life in the twentieth century. No more talents to display and polish, no more SATs, no more decisions about college or a major or a future career.

In Strat's world—now hers—this safe, enclosed, velvet world, there was only one decision. Marriage.

Her heart was so large, so aching, she needed to support it in her hands. Or Strat's. "I love you too," she told him. They were engulfed in tears: a glaze of happiness instead of sorrow.

"Why, there's Jeb!" cried Devonny, kneeling on the opposite sofa to see out the windows. "Excuse me, Stephens, I must speak to Jeb. Don't let the train leave yet."

Stephens had to lower special gleaming brass steps so that Devonny could get off. Leaning off the stairs himself, he thrust his hand high to signal the locomotive about the pause. "You look as if you're giving a benediction, Stephens," said Devonny, giggling. "Jeb! Come here! Talk to me!"

A startled Jeb turned from boarding a coach. "Miss Stratton," he said. He flushed and stumbled toward her, dragging a big shabby case held together with thin rope. He could not meet her eyes. "I have to leave, Miss Stratton. You have to understand. People are laughing at me for being such a fool, stepping out with some Irish girl that kills people."

"But Jeb—" said Devonny.

"I just said good-bye to her in the jail, that was the right thing to do, I've done right by her," he said defiantly, as if Devonny might argue, "and now I'm off to California."

"In jail?" repeated Devonny. "Bridget's in jail?"

"Of course she's in jail," said Jeb, thinking that rich women were invariably also stupid women.

"Right now she's in jail?" said Devonny.

Stephens said, "Miss Stratton. The train must leave. You must step back into the car. Now."

But Devonny Stratton jumped down onto the platform instead, yanking her voluminous skirt after her. "Strat!" she bellowed, like a farmhand. Jeb on the platform and Stephens in the private car doorway stared at her. "Strat!" shrieked Devonny. "Miss Lockwood! Walk! Get off the train! Now! We cannot leave! We are not going into New York. Father lied. Bridget is still in jail. We must rescue her forthwith!"

Mr. Rowwells set his sherry on the little writing table.

His mustache needed to be trimmed. Its little black hairs curled down over his upper lip and entered his mouth, as if they planned to grow over his teeth. I cannot kiss him, thought Harriett. I don't care if I am going to be a spinster. I don't care how great the scandal is. I shall break off my engagement to him. I will not be capital. I will marry for love or I will not marry.

Far below them spread the world of the Strattons: groomed, manicured, wrapped in blue water. She could see Mr. Stratton getting out of the carriage onto the first green. He never walked when he could ride, not even on the golf course.

Thank goodness for gloves. Harriett felt the need for layers between them.

They talked of Mr. Rowwells' world: groceries and money, new kinds of groceries, and increasing amounts of money. He talked of his hopes for mayonnaise in jars and perhaps pickles and tomato catsup as well. Harriett was not surprised that it would take a tremendous amount of capital to start such an enterprise.

That's what I am. I am only money. And even that is not good enough for Strat.

She could not be angry at Clarence Rowwells. There were limited ways in which to raise capital, and marrying a rich woman was one. He had seen his chance to slip into her favor while Strat was mooning over Miss Lockwood. One hint that he thought her pretty; one hint was all it took.

His big hairy hand removed her hat, feeling her hair and her earlobes and her throat. He nauseated her, and she said, "I wish you to do something for your bride."

"My dear. Anything."

"I wish you to save Bridget."

Mr. Rowwells stared at her. His hand ceased its movements, lying heavy and hot like a punishment.

"You are wrong that nobody cares about an Irish maid," said Harriet. "I care."

His big hairy hand came alive again, stroking her throat. It fingered the little hollow where her cameo lay on its thin gold chain, and she had the horrible thought that he might rip the cameo off her. A queer vibrating emotion seemed to come up from him, like vapor from a swamp. She fought off unreasonable fears.

"You can do it quite easily, Mr. Rowwells," she said, envying him so for being a man. "You know what happened, Mr. Rowwells."

His stare grew cold, like a winter wind. "I know what happened?" he repeated.

Inside her gloves, her hands too grew cold. They seemed to be on two sides of the same words, and she did not know why his side was so cold and frightening. "With Matthew," she said. She gathered her courage to say an insulting thing to her future husband. "Mr. Rowwells, I know why you lied."

He had lied, of course, because Mr. Stratton, the murderer, had told him to. That must have been part of the deal to get a favorable marriage settlement. Mr. Rowwells would accuse Bridget. Nobody would question the word of a gentleman, and nobody would question Mr. Stratton. Mr. Stratton was the murderer, so lying made Mr. Rowwells his accomplice. An unfortunate decision, but not irrevocable.

An extremely odd smile decorated Mr. Rowwells' face, as if painted there, as clouds were painted on the blue ceiling. She was afraid of the smile, afraid of the way he loomed over her. Afraid, even, of the way he tipped the little glass of sherry past his hairy-rimmed lips.

"Sherry," she whispered. "Sherry! You were the one for whom the tray was carried. Matthew was taking *you* sherry. *You* are—*you* are—"

He was the murderer.

She had betrothed herself to a murderer.

Not Mr. Stratton, after all, but his houseguest, Mr. Rowwells.

Harriett's emotions came back. The sense of defeat vanished and the heat exhaustion dropped away like clothes to the floor.

"Well! That settles that!" She flounced her heavy skirts, each hand lifting the hems, preparing to descend the curling stairs. "You and I will have an excursion this afternoon after all!"

Harriett was filled with relief, and even joy. I don't have to marry him! she realized. What an excuse! Nobody has to marry a murderer!

"We shall go to the police station, Mr. Rowwells," she said triumphantly. I don't have to fantasize about dying in childbirth, I can go to college, and Florinda is right, I need not marry. "You, Mr. Rowwells, will be a gentleman and admit your activities! Whatever Matthew did to annoy you, and however much it was an accident that you struck him so hard, you have a civic duty to discharge. And apologies to make to Bridget! You—"

Mr. Rowwells' heavy hand remained on her throat. The fat, splayed fingers took a different, stronger position. "I think not," he said.

"A gentleman—" said Harriett.

"Do you truly believe that the rules of gentlemanly behavior apply when the gentleman is a killer?"

The sun glittered on the open tower windows. The breeze came warm and salty on her cheeks. The sound of splashing water and the cries of triumph on the golf course reached her ears.

"Harriett, my dear, if I have thrown one down the stairs, why would I pause at throwing another?"

CHAPTER 13

Annie loved that: *forthwith*. It sounded like troops coming to the rescue. Devonny was going to be a wonderful sister-in-law.

"Bridget is still in jail?" said Strat. "But Father said—"

"This is ridiculous," said Walker Walkley, shouldering Stephens out of his way. "Devonny, get back on the train this instant. We are not disrupting our schedules because of a serving girl."

"A serving girl you lied about, Walker Walkley!" yelled Devonny. "Hiram Stratton, Jr.! Get off the train with me!"

A hundred heads popped out a hundred open coach windows as ordinary passengers delighted in the scene.

"I suggest we continue into the city," said Walk, trying to convey this opinion in all directions.

If only we could, thought Strat. Annie will be in danger if I do what Devonny wants, and that is the last thing on earth I want. But we do have to get Bridget out of jail. I cannot let her languish there, nor go on trial, not when I believe Florinda's story. But what if they put Annie in jail instead of Bridget?

He looked desperately back at his century changer. She had taken off the hat and veil. Cascades of dark hair, romantic as silk, fell toward him, and her beautiful mouth trembled, the way a girl's should, needing him.

"Come, Strat," said Walker Walkley. "Get your sister to behave and let's get this train moving. We must not have a scene."

"Walk, did you know Father lied about getting Bridget out of jail?"

"Of course."

"Why didn't you tell me?"

"I thought you knew. All the gentlemen knew."

Strat was beginning to wonder about this word gentlemen. It was supposed to mean good manners, good birth and good upbringing. "You lied too, then," he accused his friend.

"It wasn't really a lie," said Walk irritably. "It was a reasonable action. Your father didn't bother with Florinda's silliness because it meant nothing. Of course Bridget killed Matthew. If Bridget didn't, then who did?" demanded Walk.

"Mr. Rowwells killed him," said Miss Lockwood softly. "He and Ada together. They were both standing there. I was coming through time when the murder

188

happened. It's confused for me. I remember the scent of Mr. Rowwells' pipe: apples and autumn. I remember the rasping of blackness. Silk on silk, I realized later."

"Ada's shawl!" cried Devonny. "It always makes that sneaky sliding sound."

"They struck Matthew down gladly," said Anna Sophia.

"Mr. Stratton," said Stephens, "the train must leave the station. Now. You must sort out your difficulties on the platform, or in the car, sir, but not both."

"Right," said Strat. He lifted Anna Sophia to the ground.

Stephens shrugged, the brass steps were pulled up and the train pulled out of the station. Only Jeb left the village. Robert, who had not even had time to depart from the station, brought the carriage around.

Walker Walkley tried to think this through. Walk did not care for risk; the thing was to make others take the risks. The thing was to stay popular with those who had the power. At school, Strat had had the power; here, Mr. Stratton had it. How was Mr. Stratton going to react to all this coming through time nonsense? Whose side should Walk be on? Would he be better off trying to impress Devonny, Strat or Mr. Stratton? Whose friendship would prove more fruitful?

" 'Gladly,' Anna Sophia? Do you mean that?" Devonny was shocked. "They enjoyed killing him? But why? Why would they want him dead at all, let alone enjoy it?"

"This is utter nonsense," said Walk. "No gentleman would bother that much over a servant. I refuse to believe Mr. Rowwells had anything to do with it. You females are always having the vapors."

"I," said Annie, "have never experienced a vapor in my life. And I never will."

As Annie, this was true: she had never had the vapors. But as Anna Sophia, it was a lie: she *had* had the vapors. When I came back through time, she thought, I should've stopped the carriage right there on the estate and told Strat everything I remembered and trusted him to follow through. But I got vapored, thinking about how I might be hung.

She tried to figure out the rules, if any, of time travel. But all her rules had been broken, even the basics, like gravity. She didn't know whether she could save herself, *and* have both sides of time, *and* keep everybody safe, *and* still end up happily ever after.

"And as for being a gentleman, Walker Walkley," said Devonny, "you lied about Bridget making advances to you. *You* tried to yank *her* clothes off, didn't you, and when she fought you off and escaped, you decided to take revenge, didn't you?"

"She's only a maid," said Walk testily. "Who cares?"

Strat was stunned. He and Walk had both been brought up to believe that honor mattered. Both had memorized that famous poem *I could not love you, dear, so much, loved I not honor more.* And Walk had dispensed with honor? Had lied to hurt an innocent girl? A girl who rightly tried to protect her virtue?

Hiram Stratton, Jr., came out of the trance that had held him in its grip. It was amazing, really, how clouded he'd been by the love and the loss of Anna

Sophia Lockwood. He had not been paying attention for ten days.

"Come," he said. "Devonny. Annie. Get in the carriage. We're going home. We have been thinking of Bridget and Anna Sophia, but first there is Harriett. Harriett is betrothed to a murderer. She might even be alone with him now. He wouldn't hurt her, since he needs her money. We'll extricate Harriett from whatever has been signed and deal with Clarence Rowwells. Father doesn't want Harriett wed to Rowwells. He'll be delighted to prove Rowwells a murderer."

Walk shifted opinions on everything and hurried to open the carriage door for the ladies as Robert mounted to the driver's seat. Now that Strat was talking so firmly, his was a better side to be on.

"You're not coming, Walk," said Strat. "You are no longer welcome in our house."

Walk stared at his friend. "You cannot think more of an Irish maid than of me!"

"I can."

"Strat, I'm your best friend! This will blow over. We'll forget about it."

"I won't forget about it. There has been too much lying. A servant in my house is helpless, and instead of protecting her in her helplessness, we use it against her. And call ourselves gentlemen."

You *are* a gentleman, thought Annie. How she loved him, ready to do the right thing for the right reasons!

"But Strat, I have no money," said Walk desperately. "I have no place to go."

But Strat did not believe him, because Strat did not know worlds without money, could not imagine worlds without money, and assumed Walker Walkley would simply blend into another mansion with another heir and never even miss an evening bath.

Strat got into the carriage with his sister and the girl he loved, and closed the door on the whining desperation of his best friend.

"Good riddance," said Devonny. She yanked the gold cords that closed the drapes, and the sight of Walker Walkley standing in the dust was hidden forever.

But horses are slow, and time, which such power, went on without them.

"Harriett, my dear," said Clarence Rowwells, "the papers are signed. Your guardian signed them for you. Although you do not have a will, you are affianced to me. In the event of your sad demise, your money will come to me anyway." How he smiled. How his mustache crawled down into his mouth, as if it were growing longer this very minute, and taking root.

"This will actually work better, Harriett. I will have the fortune without the bother of marriage."

Harriett pressed her back against the glass window walls of the tower. "Why? I cannot understand. Why kill Matthew? Why kill me?"

"My dear Miss Ranleigh, I made a fortune in lumber, and I purchased a vast house and a fine yacht, and I lost the rest gambling. I cannot keep up pretenses much longer, especially not in front of a man so keen as Hiram Stratton. Ada and I agreed we would prevent your marriage to young Stratton so that I might have you instead. We, after all, would enjoy your money so much more than young Stratton would. I paid Ada, of course. Ada's task was simply not to chaperon you."

So Harriett had been right, down on the veranda asking for lemonade and wondering about the truth. Ada had become independent. I could have given her money, thought Harriett. I could have paid her a salary. Why did I never think of such a thing?

Harriett had detested having Ada around all the time, but it had not crossed her mind how much Ada must detest being around Harriett all the time.

Mr. Rowwells was afraid but proud of himself. There was a great deal at stake here; Harriett could see the gambler in him. Everything on one throw. But the throw was her own life.

"Ada and I planned that I would compromise your virtue, if necessary, so you would be forced to wed me. Oh, we had many plans. But none were needed. You poor, plain, bucktoothed, mousy-haired fool, you listened when I told you that the moonlight made you pretty."

Even through her terror, the description hurt. She guessed that he had told Ada she was attractive too, and such is the desire of women to be beautiful that toothless, wrinkled, despairing Ada had warmed to him also.

Tears spilled from Harriett's eyes. I don't want to be

plain! I didn't want to live out my life plain, and I don't want to die plain.

"And then Miss Lockwood fell from the sky, as it were. Where did she come from? It was most mysterious, her coming and her going. But so useful. She removed young Stratton from the scene in one evening and you were mine instead." He seemed regretful, all those fine plans for nothing.

"Did you kill Miss Lockwood too?" said Harriett. "Is that how she vanished so completely? Did you or Ada drown her in the pond?"

"You would have liked that, wouldn't you? Jealous, weren't you?" said Mr. Rowwells. "No, I don't know what happened to the beautiful little Lockwood. But I didn't mind that young Stratton went insane over her loss. Any Stratton loss is a gain of mine."

She had begun trembling, and he could certainly see it. Her body, face, mouth, all were shivering. She was ashamed of the extent of her fear. I cannot die a coward, she thought. I must think of a way to fight back.

She tried to stave him off. "But where does Matthew come into it?"

Rowwells shrugged. How massive his shoulders were. How fat, like sausages, were his fingers. The corset, tied so tightly by Ada herself this morning, hardly gave Harriett enough breath to cry out with, let alone hit and fight, and rush down the stairs, and not get caught.

"Prior to Miss Lockwood's arrival, prior to young Stratton's feverish excitement that blinded him to you,

Matthew overheard us planning what I would do to you in the carriage. The details would only distress you, and one scrap of me is a gentleman still, so I shall omit the details. Ada, however, felt it would be quite easy to make you believe you had to marry quickly, or else have a child out of wedlock."

She closed her eyes. What rage, what hate Ada must have felt in order to make such plans. Toward *me,* thought Harriett, unable to believe it. But I am a nice person!

"Matthew, unfortunately, was not willing to accept money." Clarence Rowwells was still incredulous. What human being would choose anything other than money? "Matthew," said Mr. Rowwells, as if it still angered him, as if he, Rowwells, had been in the right, "Matthew said he would go straight to Mr. Stratton with the conversation." Mr. Rowwells actually looked to Harriett for understanding. "What could I do?" he said, as if he, a rich, articulate man, had been helpless. "I had to stop Matthew. I chased after him, arguing, offering him more money, and there he was, stalking down the stairs as if *he* were the gentleman!"

Clarence Rowwells was outraged. Matthew had dared to act as if he knew best! "Matthew was taking the tray back to the kitchen," said Mr. Rowwells, "and he would not stop when I instructed him to. I grabbed him and slammed him against the stair tread and that was that." He dusted himself, as if Matthew had been lint on his jacket.

Well, thought Harriett, I know one thing. I would actually rather be dead than be married to Clarence

Rowwells. And I know, too, why Ada feels independent. What could Clarence Rowwells do now except pay her forever? All she need do is stay away from stairwells and towers.

The man's chest was rising and falling as he nervously sucked in air. He does not want to hurt me, she thought. How can I talk him out of this? How can I convince him to let me go? "Nobody will believe there could be two violent deaths in as many weeks," she said. "They will know I could not have fallen by accident."

"This is true," he agreed. His hands, like wood blocks, shifted from her throat to her waist, and placed her solidly on the rosebud carved stool in front of the tiny desk. "It was no accident, though," he said. "Poor Harriett. So in love with young Mr. Stratton, heartsick at finding herself about to wed a man she does not love. A fiancé," he said almost bitterly, "that she does not even like to look at."

So he too had feelings which had been hurt. He too had wanted to be told he was attractive. But that hardly gave him the right to do away with her.

With a giddy sarcasm, he went on. "This sweet young woman chooses to hurl herself off the tower instead. What a wrenching letter she leaves behind! How guilty young Strat feels. How people weep at the funeral." He dipped the pen in the inkwell and handed it to her.

"You cannot make me write!" cried Harriett.

He shrugged. "Then I will pen it myself. I write a

fine hand, Miss Ranleigh. Prepare to meet your Maker."

The glass broke.

A thousand shards leaped into the air, like rainbows splintering from the heat of the sun.

CHAPTER 14

The gun smoked.

"Really, I feel quite faint," said Florinda. "Harriett, you must never go unchaperoned. Look at the sort of things that happen. Men try to throw you out of towers." Florinda's lavender silk gown was hardly ruffled, and her hair was still coiled in perfect rolls. Her lace glove was covered with gunpowder. Florinda said, "Mr. Rowwells, I suggest you sit on the window seat before you bleed to death. Harriett, I suggest you descend the stairs. Mind your skirt as you pass me. Use the telephone. You have my permission. Summon the police."

"I miss all the good stuff!" moaned Devonny. "Florinda shoots a murderer and I'm not even here! Life is so unfair."

"I could shoot him again for you," said Florinda. "I didn't hit him in a fatal place the first time."

The young people collapsed laughing. Mr. Stratton did not. Discovering that he was married to a woman who shot people when they got in the way was quite appalling.

"He was about to throw me off the tower," said Harriett. "He thought I knew that he was the murderer. Of course I didn't know. I just thought his lies were because—" she caught herself in time. She didn't want Mr. Stratton to know she had thought *he* was the murderer.

"I," said Florinda, "had thought of nothing else since I realized it could not be Bridget. The only odd thing I could come up with was that Ada never chaperoned Harriett when she was with Mr. Rowwells. What a strange decision on her part. Then I noticed that Ada had new clothes. She hasn't worn them. They are maroon and wine silk instead of black. She was celebrating something. Going somewhere. I decided to sit on the stairs beneath the tower and be Harriett's chaperon. Luckily, Mr. Rowwells wasted time telling Harriett why he killed Matthew. Time enough for me to fly to the gun room and get the pistol."

Annie was awestruck. She herself would have used the telephone, summoning professional rescuers. She would have dialed 911, saying, Please! Come! Help! Save me!

"Call the newspapers!" said Devonny. "We want to brag about Florinda. Nobody else has a stepmother who gets rid of evil fiancés."

"We will not call the papers," said Mr. Stratton. What was the world coming to? His women were behaving like men. He chomped cigars and sipped brandy, but neither helped. "The doctor has removed the bullet and bandaged the arm. Mr. Rowwells will recover."

"What a shame," said Devonny, meaning it. "Florinda, we should take up target practice."

"Why? Who are *you* planning to shoot?" said Florinda.

"Stop this!" shouted Mr. Stratton. "I am beside myself!"

Beside myself, thought Annie. Now that I'm a century changer, I hear more. Is Mr. Stratton really beside himself? Is he a second person now, standing next to the flesh of the real person, but no longer living in it?

It is Ada who is beside herself, she thought. Poor, poor Ada. Living a dark and loveless life, swathed in black thoughts, willing to do anything to rescue herself. And now she has done anything, and life is even worse. She has Bridget's cell; she has inherited the rats and the filth.

She found herself aching for Ada. If time had trapped anybody, it was Ada. What might she have done, with a car and a college degree and a chance?

"We must try to lessen the scandal," said Mr. Stratton severely. "I require that joking about these matters cease."

But his requirements were not of interest to his son, daughter and wife, and after a few more minutes of confusion, he retreated to his library before the next round of giggles began.

Mr. Stratton would never understand females. He had generously had Robert collect Bridget and bring her back to the Mansion. But the maid was at this moment in her attic room packing. Now that he'd given her back her position, what was she doing? Going to Texas! On money Florinda had demanded he give the girl!

Why Texas? Devonny had asked.

Because Jeb's taken California, said the girl.

Whereupon Florinda commanded Hiram to allow Matthew's wife and five children to remain in the stable apartment! Hiram Stratton was very uncomfortable with the way Florinda was making things happen. It wasn't ladylike.

But the vision he would keep forever would be the sight of Ada, spitting, shrieking obscenities, kicking and biting. The lady he had kept in his home to teach Harriett and Devonny how to be ladies was a primitive animal.

I had no money, she kept screaming, what did you think I would do in old age? I had to have money!

In the quiet smoky dark of his library, Mr. Stratton thought that perhaps Harriett and Devonny should go to college after all. Perhaps women—and education—and money—

But it was too difficult a thought to get hold of, so Mr. Stratton had a brandy instead.

*   *   *

Time was also the subject elsewhere in the Mansion.

"Let's all hold hands and time travel together," said Devonny. "I want to visit the court of Queen Elizabeth the First."

"It doesn't work that way," said Annie. She did not want them joking about it. It was too intense, too terrifying, too private, for jokes.

"How does it work?" asked Harriett. She was astonished to find that Strat was holding her hand. She wore no gloves, nor did he, and the warmth and tightness of his grip was the most beautiful thing that had ever happened to her. Harriett knew he was just reassuring himself that she really was all right. She tried not to let herself slip into believing that he loved her after all. The worst punishment, she thought, will be leaving my heart in his hands, when his heart is elsewhere.

"I don't know how it works," said Annie.

"It must take a terrible toll on your body to fall a hundred years," said Devonny.

Miss Lockwood's body looked fine to Harriett.

"Did you touch something?" said Devonny. "Perhaps we should try to touch everything in the whole Mansion and make wishes at the same time."

Miss Lockwood shook her head. "No, because remember, the second time I traveled, we weren't in the Mansion, we were out on the road, you were in the carriage."

"Was it true love that brought you through?" cried Florinda, clasping her hands together romantically.

"Strat, was your heart crying out? Or Anna Sophia, was yours?"

My heart was the one crying out for true love, thought Harriett. It's *still* crying out. It will *always* cry out.

Harriett too saw Ada as she had been when the police took her away. In the midst of the obscenities and the drooling fury at being caught Ada had the very same heart that all women had. Ada had cried out for decades trying to get love. She had settled for money. She had had time to buy a few dresses and dream of a rail ticket. But it was Bridget, after all, who would take the journey.

"Mr. Rowwells told his attorney that he and Ada actually wondered if they had summoned you from another world, Miss Lockwood," said Florinda.

"I wondered that too. Did somebody summon me? Did somebody need me for something special? But if they did, I failed them and it," said Miss Lockwood.

Harriett could admire Miss Lockwood as simply a creature of beauty. She could see how much more easily all things would come to a girl who looked like that. Including love. How cruel, how viciously cruel, then, to let a woman be born plain.

"As for Ada," said Devonny, "I cannot believe Ada has special powers. If she did, she would have used them to get money years ago, or time travel herself to a better place, or fly away from the police when they took her this afternoon."

This afternoon.

It was still this same afternoon.

Truly, time was awesome. So much could be packed into such a tiny space! Lives could change forever in such short splinters of time.

Bridget came up timidly, her possessions packed in canvas drawstring, like the laundry bags in Strat's boarding school.

Florinda hugged her. "I apologize for the men in my household, Bridget."

"I accept your apology," said Bridget. She had lovely new clothes that had been Miss Devonny's, and the heavy weight of silver pulled her skirt pocket down. More than anything, she was glad to be clean, glad to have spent an hour in Miss Florinda's bath.

"Texas!" said Florinda. "I'm so excited for you."

Florinda is trapped, thought Bridget, by her husband and fashions and society. Florinda can only dream of the adventures that I will have.

"Go and be brave," whispered Florinda, and Bridget saw that behind the vapors and the fashion, the veils and perfumes, was a strong woman with no place in which to be strong.

But it was Harriett who muffled a sob. Florinda swept Harriett up, hiding the weeping face inside her own lacy sleeves.

What have I done! thought Annie Lockwood, so ashamed she wanted to hide her own face. I've waltzed into these people's lives, literally—I waltzed in the ruined ballroom, waltzed down the century, waltzed in Strat's arms—and I destroyed them. I took their lives and wrenched them apart. For the person who needs to go and be brave is Harriett, and I don't think she can. Not without Strat.

Bridget swung her canvas bag onto her shoulder. Poor Harriett. Bridget had never attended school, but she'd walked into the village school a few times, when there were special events. It looked like such fun. You and your friends, sitting in rows and learning and laughing, singing and spelling.

Bridget could spell nothing.

And what good had it done Harriett to be able to spell everything? To read everything and write everything? She was just another desperate woman weeping because she had no man's loving arms to hold her.

But Strat, being a man, was too thick to know that he was the cause of the tears. "You are exhausted, Harriett," he said immediately. "You must rest. There has been too much emotion in this day for you."

The ladies smiled gently, forgiving him for being a man and too dense to understand.

"Write to me, Bridget," whispered Florinda over Harriett's bowed head.

Bridget smiled. Of course she could not write to Florinda. She could not write.

"Good-bye," she said, and Bridget went, and was brave.

The setting sun fell, and a long thin line of gold lay quiet on the water. Dusk slipped in among them. The carriage taking Bridget back to the station clattered heavily down the lanes of the Stratton estate.

Strat bade Harriett and Devonny and Florinda good night, and took Miss Lockwood on his arm. They walked the long way through the gardens, out of view of the veranda. The moon rose, its delicate light a silver edge to every leaf.

"I love you," she said. "I will always love you." Her throat filled with a terrible final agony. *I could not love you, dear, so much, loved I not honor more.* Somehow I've got to love honor more than Strat. I have to be a better person than Miss Bartten.

Annie had tasted both sides of time, and each in its way was so cruel to women. But she must not be one of the women who caused cruelty; she must be one who eased it. "I can't stay, Strat," she whispered.

"Yes, you can!" He was shocked, stunned. "That's why you came back! You love me! That's how you traveled, I know it is, it was love! Anna Sophia, you—"

"Marry Harriett," she said.

He stood very still. Their hands were still entwined, but he was only partly with her now.

"I love *you,*" whispered Strat.

But she understood now that love was not always part of the marriages these people made. He was affectionate toward Harriett, and would be kind to her; Harriett needed Strat; that was enough.

And my mother and father? she thought. What will be enough for them?

She'd cast her parents aside without a moment's thought when she changed centuries. But they were still there, going on with their lives, aching and hurting because of each other, aching and hurting because of their daughter.

"I've been cruel," she said. "To you and to my parents, to Harriett and to Sean. And I'm going to be punished for it. Time is going to leave my heart here with you, while my body will go on. I was thinking what power I had, but really, the power belongs to Time." She touched his odd clothes, the funny big collar, the soft squashy tie, the heavy turned seams. Cloth—in this century, always cloth that you could touch. And only cloth that you could touch. "Oh, Strat, it's going to be the worst punishment! I'm going to leave my heart in your century and then have to go occupy my body in the next."

He looked glazed. He too clung, but for him the cloth was nothing; he neither saw it nor felt it. "Annie, I love you. If you stay with me," he promised, "I'll take care of you forever. You'll never have to make another decision. I'll protect you from everything."

He had made the finest offer he knew how to make.

And on his side of time, his side of the century, how could he know how unattractive the offer was? For Annie wanted to be like Bridget, and see the world, and make her own way and take her own risks. Every choice made for her? It was right for Harriett, but it would never be right for Annie.

"No, Strat. I love you. And I care about Harriett and Devonny and all that they are or could be. So I'm going."

Her tears slipped down her cheeks, and he kissed them, as if he could kiss away the desperation they shared. And then, hesitating still, he kissed her lips. She knew that she would never have such a kiss again, in his world or in hers. It was a kiss of love, a kiss that tried to keep her, a kiss that tried so hard to seal a bargain she could not make.

A kiss in which she knew she would never meet a finer man.

Miss Bartten had this same moment, thought Annie, this fraction in Time where she could have said, No, we're stopping, I won't be the woman who hurts others.

Oh, Strat, you are a good man. And I know you will be good to Harriett, who needs you.

Annie, who had wanted that kiss the most, and dreamed of it most, was the one to stop the kiss.

"I need something of yours to take with me," she told him, sobbing. Her tears were unbearable to him, and he pulled out his handkerchief, a great linen square with his initials fatly embroidered in one corner. It was enough. She had this of Strat, and could leave.

"I'm going," she said to Strat, and knew that she did control at least some of Time. She was a Century Changer, and in her were powers given to very few. *I love you, Strat,* said her heart.

"No!" he cried.

The last sound she heard from Strat's side of Time was his howl of grief, and the last thing she felt were his strong fingers, not half so strong as Time.

Her heart fell first, going without her, stripped and in pain, the loss of Strat like the end of the world.

She was a leaf in a tornado, ripped so badly she could not believe she would emerge alive.

The spinning was deeper and more horrific than the other times. There were faces in it with her: terrible, unknown, screaming faces of others being wrenched through Time.

I am not the only changer of centuries. And they are all as terrified and powerless as I.

Her mind was blown away like the rest of her.

It learned only one thing, as it was thrown, and that was even more frightening than leaving her heart with Strat.

She was going *down*. Home was *up*. Home was future years, not past years! *Down through Time?* Was she going to some other century?

Home! *She had meant to go home.*

My family—my friends—my life—

The handkerchief was ripped from her hand. Wherever she went, whenever she landed, she would have nothing of Strat.

Strat! she screamed, but soundlessly, for the race of Time did not allow speech. Her tears were raked from her face as if by the tines of forks.

It ended.

The falling had completed itself.

She was still standing.

She was not even dizzy.

She stood very still, not ready to open her eyes, because once her eyes were open, the terrible unknown would be not *where* she was, but *when* she was.

Would it be the gift of adventure to do it again? To visit yet another century? Or would it be a terrible punishment?

Why was any of it happening, and why to Annie Lockwood?

When did she really want to find herself?

She thought of Strat and Harriett, of Devonny, Florinda, and Bridget . . . and again of Strat. Will I ever know what happened to them?

She thought of her mother and father, brother and boyfriend, school and girlfriends. I *have* to know what happens to them!

She opened her eyes to see when, and what, came next.

CAROLINE B. COONEY is the author of many novels for young adults, including *Driver's Ed; The Face on the Milk Carton* (an IRA-CBC Children's Choice Book); its companion, *Whatever Happened to Janie?* (an ALA Best Book for Young Adults); *Among Friends; The Girl Who Invented Romance; Camp Girl-Meets-Boy; Camp Reunion; Family Reunion; Don't Blame the Music* (an ALA Best Book for Young Adults); *Twenty Pageants Later;* and *Operation: Homefront.* She lives in Westbrook, Connecticut.

Reviewers praise *Driver's Ed*

☆ "A wrenching, breathlessly paced plot and an adrenaline-charged romance make Cooney's latest novel nearly impossible to put down. . . . Given Cooney's vigorous, evocative prose and her carefully individuated characters, this modern-day morality tale is as convincing as it is irresistible."
—*Publishers Weekly*, Starred

☆ "A poignant, realistic novel, with nicely drawn characters and a vintage metaphor that's actually refreshing: a driver's license . . . is the 'ticket out of childhood.'"
—*Booklist*, Starred

"Takes on sensitive issues and deals with them in a compelling manner. The overriding tension . . . will attract teens."
—*School Library Journal*

Driver's Ed was like so many things in school. If the parents only knew . . .

Remy Marland crossed her fingers and prayed to the God of Driver Education that she would get to drive today. Remy loved to drive. She did not know where she was going, but one thing was for sure. She was going to get there fast.

Morgan Campbell had been standing on the threshold of turning sixteen and getting his driver's license ever since he could remember. Deep in the first crush of his life, thinking of nothing but girls, Morgan forgot what driving was all about.

Driver's Ed . . . the only life and death course in school.